STILL WATERS

STILL WATERS
Mystery Tales of the Canals

Margaret Cornish

With Illustrations by Valerie Croker

ROBERT HALE · LONDON

Robert Hale Limited
Clerkenwell House
Clerkenwell Green
London EC1R 0HT

British Library Cataloguing in Publication Data

Cornish, Margaret
　　Still waters.
　　I. Title
823'.914 [F]

ISBN 0 7090 4015 6

Photoset by Rowland Phototypesetting Ltd
Printed in Great Britain by
St Edmundsbury Press, Bury St Edmunds, Suffolk
Bound by Woolnough Bookbinding Ltd, Northants

Contents

DEDICATION

To all boatmen and their families who worked and travelled on the narrow boats unsung and almost unheard of through over a century of English canal history.

To my friends and colleagues who continued to work the boats through the stringent war years of 1940 until 1946.

To all the enthusiasts who still work to reclaim and maintain the great network of the waterways and who strive to keep alive the old traditions of the narrow boats and the old boat people's fraternity.

Preface

The two thousand miles of quiet waterways which wind through lonely countryside and through the hearts of our busiest cities have been shocked into a revival of activity and interest by the thousands of holiday visitors who have only recently discovered a whole way of life, together with its folklore and traditions which have survived almost unknown and unchanged for the past two hundred years.

The boat people lived separate lives and worked apart from the more established and respectable citizens of their time. They were travellers like the Romany and they resented being referred to as 'gypsies' – a term often synonymous with thieves and ne'er-do-wells. Like the Romany they had their own customs and codes of behaviour, their own pride and a fierce resentment of interference from the 'outside'. They were regarded with fear and suspicion by the 'decent' town-dwellers who lived in the areas through which the canals passed. "Keep away from the Cut or the bargees will get you" was as fearsome a threat to adventure-some youngsters as the threat of Boney from across the sea.

The boat people worked hard and lived in conditions which were cramped and unsanitary by modern standards. Yet most of them brought up families, maintained a rigorous standard of cleanliness, and brought colour and warmth of living to these narrow lines of transport which thread through the towns and villages of this island.

There were tales of violence and wild behaviour, often exaggerated in the mellow warmth of the many canal-side pubs. There were superstitions and old tales associated with the long tunnels, the lonely stretches under the overhanging trees and the old, deserted quarries and buildings left to decay and crumble into the waters of the canals and rivers. No one tied up under the Spinneys after dark or by the old cement workings – anything could happen. On Hallowe'en all boats would be tied up well before dark and the cabin doors firmly closed against the night and the menacing dark.

The mystery stories in this book are based on some of these superstitions and on some of the snatches of half-remembered tales told long ago in the cosy warmth of the lamp-lit cabins and round the log fires of the old, now derelict, pubs. Perhaps they may be revived to be told again in the comfort and security of cabins lit by electricity and in pubs resplendent with souvenirs of their more humble origins.

M. Cornish
1982

The Swimming Cat

Bird song and bluebells. Green, green, the cuckoo green of spring in early June. Mayflowers dripping laden branches into the water, showering petals. "Like confetti at a wedding," thought Liz as the boat swept through them, piling them at the water's edge as they passed. "Like foam," she thought, her similes changing inconsequentially as her moods. Today, fresh, hopeful, exuberant. "It was a lover and his lass," she sang to anyone who would listen. There was no one; the steady phut-phut of the engine successfully drowned her musical inadequacies so that she continued with badly memorized snatches from schoolday

9

singing sessions. "Hey-ho and a hey-nonny-no." Hey-nonnies and la-las, inconsequential as the bird songs. A cuckoo interrupted, close enough for her to hear. "Cuckoo," she shouted back, turned to Steph on the butty and pointed, meaningless. "Cuckoo," she shouted back again and Steph waved in reply.

A good-to-be-alive day. Liz stretched her arms sideways, over her head, tiller held in the small of her back, hard knob against hard vertebrae. "Cuckoo, cuckoo-oo," she sang, changing songs as she changed metaphors, changed moods.

Yesterday, cold-wind-rain, Hatton and Knowle, endless locks, awkward rigid oilskins, sweat-rain-mud-exhaustion. Surly, withdrawn into herself she had muttered "Bugger off" when Steph had asked her to join them for a meal in the butty cabin.

Steph was a forgiving soul and she understood something of the reasons for the black moods which often threatened to engulf her friend. Liz had immediately claimed the abandoned baby, found last Christmas under the cratch of their motor-boat, for her own.* Over their Christmas drinks she had told Stephanie about Patrick, about the deliriously happy seven months they had spent together. Married at Chelsea Registry Office on a brief forty-eight hours' leave, it had been a wild, hilarious day with Patrick's friends and two of her own who were around at the time. They had wined and dined at the Coque d'Or in the King's Road, had walked and danced all the way to Trafalgar Square, gone to The Windmill, then more drinks and, finally, tearful goodbyes. The rest of the precious time had been spent behind closed curtains of the Northumberland Hotel. Patrick's squadron moved from Cambridge to Lossiemouth; Liz had no other thought than to be with Patrick and she had gone too. How quickly those seven months had passed. Then came the day that Skippy, one of their friends, came instead of Patrick and she knew that it was over. Skippy and his friends had done their best; they were marvellous.

"The blasted kite was US [unserviceable]. Should never have happened," they said; but it would have happened later if not sooner. Liz knew and they had known. The light and the gaiety had gone out of their young eyes and they were already old in the foreknowledge of their own destruction.

* *See* 'A Baby for Christmas' published in *Waterways World*, December 1976.

The baby had been born prematurely and survived only a couple of days. It was a girl. Everyone had been most kind.

Liz and Steph had talked through most of the night, first in the Black Boy and later in the warm companionship of the butty cabin. Jan, the third member of the crew, had been on leave staying with her sister and nephews in Barnet. Liz had talked briefly about her stay in the mental hospital.

"A hell-hole," she said with a shudder. "Shock treatment and drugs. So awful it scared me to death – almost. At least it cured me – I was terrified at the thought of spending my life in such a place. Finally managed to convince the doctor that I was all right, that I could manage. Told me I should quit teaching and do a hard physical job."

"So you came on the boats."

"Just by chance. Saw this ad in a magazine for women volunteers. Thought I'd give it a try and – well, here we are."

Stephanie was a good listener; her sympathy had flowed with the drinks and she had agreed that, somehow, Liz must keep the baby. After all, it was Liz who had heard the crying during the night when they had been tied up at the top of Knowle on the previous trip; neither Steph nor Jan had heard so much as a whimper.

"Heard it twice," Liz's voice slurred with the drink, the warmth of the cabin and exhaustion of spent emotion. "Heard it twice," she repeated. "Looked ever'where. Thought it was drowned in th'lock."

"We thought you were imagining it because you were so unhappy, you know."

"Obvious, was it?" Liz had replied sharply.

"Only sometimes. We thought you were getting better. And then this crying business got us worried about you."

Liz had been warmed by their forbearance, especially as neither of them had intruded upon her private grief with unwelcome questions.

"But you see, I didn't imagine it all. There's Noelle."

"Couldn't have been her all the time," Stephanie had observed.

There had been no real explanation of the wailing which Liz had heard at the top of the locks; but Noelle was real enough. There had followed all the long and tedious interviews with the police, with health and welfare workers; all the more protracted because of Liz's claim to the baby. The mother still had not been traced and the outcome was still unsettled. For the present the baby was being well cared for by a foster mother in Knowle and the girls went to see her as often as possible. A delightful bundle, eyes beginning to turn from blue to grey.

"Just like mine," Liz had proclaimed triumphantly.

"Still as determined to claim the child," thought Stephanie with a sigh. However would she manage, even with the small pension she received as a widow, if she were allowed to adopt Noelle. There were so many conditions and restrictions.

She sighed again, thinking of the problems with which her friend Liz would be faced if the adoption of Noelle was effected.

But today cuckoos were cuckooing, the sun was warm and Liz's black mood of the day before was dissipated. She waved now, hand to ear, to acknowledge the welcome cuckoo sound. They were still young and hopeful, impressionable and responsive to the mood of the moment. Steph was easy-going; later she'd be even more tolerant and understanding, a recipient of others' problems. "Sloppy, place like a tip, good-hearted though." Condescending, they'd censure to justify the inroads they made upon her time, her sympathy, her considered listening to their inconsequential outpourings. Today she read the signs; Liz was herself again; it would be an easy day with the prospect of an early tie-up in Tyseley and baths, cinema, chips and sausages; the weariness, blackness and wetness of yesterday forgotten. Steph smiled and she pulled one of the long, floppy ears of the dog she had rescued on a cold day in February. The puppy had been abandoned by a lockside with a string round its neck; it had been in the water but somehow had scrambled out. The string had bitten deeply, but Stephanie had bathed it, dried it and taken it into her bed. Candy became one of the crew but was especially devoted to Steph. She was stretched out now on the warm cabin top and turned with a look of devotion as Steph pulled at her ear. Steph smiled again. She smiled easily, mostly to herself, a reflex response when her mind was easy.

"Nice teeth, nice mouth," a young man had told her. The war 'out there' had swallowed him. She hadn't heard where he was, he hadn't written; but Steph still smiled at the memory of summer walks in Kew Gardens and at Richmond; there had been days like this with sun and fresh smells of lilac before the heady rose blossoms burdened the gardens and before the onset of the sultry summer heat which had heavied her heart when he left. They had walked together at weekends. Both had been at London University, she reading Social Sciences and he reading History, and they had talked endlessly about the courses and about the careers they hoped to follow – she as a schools' Health Visitor and he as an agent and organizer for the Labour Party in Liverpool. He had been very positive if slightly opinionated. On Saturday evenings they had danced at a student club where they had first met. Steph had lived with her parents at Watford, Keith in a flat – Pimlico – parents somewhere up north. There hadn't been time for details, for confidences, for home introductions. In July he'd been called up; said he'd write but he didn't. Steph was hurt, a little sad on the spring days; she now smiled again to herself at the memory of hand clasps, the tentative embrace as they danced, the rare chaste kisses. "A day like today," she thought as she hung over the tiller of the butty, "two years ago," and waved to Liz, smiling again at her antics on the motor. Liz had hoisted herself onto the cabin top, black hair against the black chimney, steering with a competently casual foot on the tiller; a good straight run through Catherine de Barnes – Catty Barnes the real boat people called it – to Tyseley.

"In a good mood, is she?" Jan leaned out from the butty cabin; short, busy, capable, intolerant of moods and insensitive to changes of weather and changes of temperamental response. She had been a hospital orderly; her code of conduct cleanliness, punctuality, reliability, by which she lived narrowly and judged others rigidly. Rejected by the Red Cross for active service – no qualifications from a senior school – she left the hospital in a fit of pique, saw a Ministry of Transport advertisement for boatwomen to be trained, applied and was accepted. Amazed at the acceptance, amazed at her own irrational act – hardly a considered decision – she found herself on a pair of boats with a trainer whom she slavishly admired and two other trainees whom she despised. "Feckless, lazy, hoity-toity," she branded them on the second day out from Maida Vale. The six weeks of training had toughened her stubborn streak and her determination to stick it out to prove herself to the trainer and to show the other two that she could take it. They left before the end of the second trip much to her gratification.

Liz and Steph both thought of her as a gift as neither liked the chores of cleaning. She scrubbed the decks daily, polished brasses and kept the exteriors of the boats spotless. She left the motor cabin severely alone. "It's revolting, never gives it a good scrub, but that's her affair; she has to live in it." The constant comment of scorn boosted her self-esteem. Liz was by far the better boatwoman; Jan's judgement was often faulty. The other two forbore to comment when Jan's steering led them into difficulties or when she jammed the boats in a lock. Liz swore only on her bad days, but that could be often enough and, whenever possible, Jan contented herself with lock-wheeling, cleaning and cooking. Liz preferred to take the motor; she was steerer after all and hers the ultimate responsibility for working the boats, for keeping the crew together. A steerer could soon get a bad name on the Cut. "Drives herself, drives everyone . . . bad-tempered . . . lazy slut . . ." The word would go around and crews be difficult to find. Liz was known to be moody, but Steph and Jan had stayed with her for almost a year. She was a capable boatwoman and her lighter side was delightful. "An odd job lot," she had said, "but we fit together pretty well." They felt complacent when they thought of the comings and goings – mostly goings – of other crews, wartime volunteers with no compulsion to endure the hard winter months.

Now it was summer, squally but warm enough to work more easily in blouses, pullovers and dungarees, with old school plimsolls to replace the heavy working men's boots bought without coupons down Commercial Road. Jan emerged into the well-deck, brasso and rags in hand. The chimney brasses shone in the sunlight but to Jan the daily round of cleaning was imperative. Her squat, square hands, tanned and nail-bitten, unscrewed the cap. Liz had stopped 'mucking about', as she put it; a bridge 'ole was ahead and Liz always gave bridge 'oles her full attention. Steph rowed the great tiller slowly to keep the butty's bows in line. Jan was busy with the chimney brasses. Suddenly a burst of thick black smoke ejected from the exhaust chimney on the motor; the silence was ominous as the engine died and the bows of the motor swung slowly over towards the far bank. Steph pushed the butty tiller hard to brake on the mud, towpath side.

Liz had stepped off, slipped a cotton line over the back stud to hold in the stern; she looked back disconsolate, exuberance extinguished.

"Something in the blades," she shouted. Steph was on the cabin roof of the butty and along the top planks to the for'ard deck. It was quite a leap to the bank; she just made it one foot slipping back into the wet mud. Jan, less agile, made no attempt to follow, but pulled out the tiller to stop it swinging, lodged it in the hatch and continued to polish.

"Could be anything," said Liz, her voice flat, dispirited. "You know this stretch. Bed springs, bicycles, prams, sacks, old rope, anything."

"I'll have the first prod." Steph, helpful as always, took the short shaft while Liz held the stern as rigid as possible pulling on the cotton line and pushing away with the mop.

Steph prodded. "Soggy . . . solid," she muttered, hooking and pulling.

"Want any help?" shouted Jan from the butty. Liz shook her head. "Cocoa," she added as an afterthought.

Steph had hooked something. "Can't move it." She pulled again, then pushed. "Soft . . . but tough . . . a sack . . . an old coat. May have to go in."

"Not on this stretch." Liz looked at the oily black water and shivered. She had been in often enough to saw and hack the coils of wire and ends of old ropes which wrapped themselves inextricably round the shaft of the blades; the stretch from there to Tyseley through the outskirts of Brummagem was filthy, a refuse tip for kids from nearby housing estates. There were rumours too of bodies.

"Could be a body." Steph stopped pulling; the idea had crossed her mind as well. They looked at each other with sick horror at the possibility.

"Here, I'll have a go." Liz took the shaft, pushed and turned so that the hook was well caught. She braced her feet against an edge of the stone coping where the cinder path had broken away, then leaned back and pulled.

Bubbles . . . more bubbles.

"Coming," she shouted as she felt the shaft slowly drag away from the blades. She closed her eyes with the effort. Another push, twist and pull. There was a sudden scream from Steph.

"Bodies," she yelled. "Kittens . . . oh . . . horrible."

They floated one after another, bloated, shapeless, bald; bloodless entrails dangling where the shaft had hooked them. They floated obscenely round the motor's counter.

Liz dropped the shaft, looked and froze, felt the nausea rising. Steph looked away but picked up the shaft before it slithered back over the edge of the coping. She grabbed the cotton line, stood on it and wrenched viciously with the shaft. It gave, a large remnant of sacking attached. Keeping as far back as possible she dragged the sodden shapeless remains onto the bank. She heard Liz being sick on the bank behind her.

"All right?" shouted Jan. "Cocoa's ready. Come across, no boats coming."

There was no answer. Something wrong? She put the steaming mugs on the cabin top, prepared to heave her dumpy form up through the hatchway. She bent down to fix a loose shoelace; a moving streak through the water on the offside of the well-deck caught her eye. A rat. She looked again. A large rat.

"It's a cat," she said aloud. Wild-eyed, fur streaked, swimming with head and shoulders held high it swam level, a foot or two from the boatside.

Jan was short, she'd never reach it. She grabbed the other home-made rag mop and thrust it in front of the wretched animal, but it swerved turning in a half-circle round the end of the rudder making for the bank. "Mud," thought Jan, "it will never make it." She levered the short plank, softly not to frighten further the already frantic creature, until the end of it rested lightly on the mud at the edge of the bank and as near to the cat as possible. The animal was tiring; sinking front paws scraped the end of the solid plank; with an effort it scrabbled further until it was clear of the water. It crouched there, fur spiked and sodden, tail whippy like a rat's; black with white patches, a white snarl near the nose, common enough. Candy had retreated to the shelter of the cabin – growling apprehensively as she slunk down the steps.

"Puss . . . puss . . . come on puss," Jan called hopefully. She didn't like cats but she couldn't watch one drown.

It remained there crouching on the end of the plank, made no attempt to move, while Jan still held the other end across the side of the boat.

"Help, I've got a cat," she called. "Steph, come and give me a

16

hand." There was no response. Steph still seemed to be tugging away at whatever it was. Liz was being sick, which struck Jan as odd – Liz was never sick. Her attention was focused on the cat; it opened its mouth as if to mew but no sound came.

"Come *on* puss." Jan was impatient; she felt needed up for'ard. Damn the cat. She pulled in the plank as smoothly as she could; the cat arched its back digging frenzied claws into the wood. Suddenly it leapt into the boat, tense and shaking. Jan shoved the plank along the cabin top, grabbed a piece of cleaning rag and made to pick up the cat to dry off some of the gritty water. The cat glared, hissed, leapt again, just missed the steaming mugs and made off into the hold out of sight. Candy yelped and shivered in the far corner of the cabin.

"Please yourself," muttered Jan, dismissing the cat as it was now obvious that something was amiss under the bridge. "Bad-tempered bugger." She only swore when alone. "Swearing lets you down," she thought privately. Her dad swore all the time. When Liz swore she was diminished in Jan's opinion. Steph never swore; Jan thought her upbringing as a minister's daughter had something to do with it.

Something *was* wrong. "Want some help?" she called. She'd only risk the top planks in an emergency.

Steph walked back along the towpath.

"Kittens," she said, coming alongside. "A sack of kittens, drowned; sack must have been floating just below the surface. Caught on the prop. Horrible. Liz has been sick." She looked pretty grey herself.

"I'll bring the cocoa along," said Jan, fear of top planks gone in the need to help her mates.

"I'll help Liz to start up again. Boats might come." Steph turned back to the bridge.

Jan hoisted herself, picked up two mugs, carefully walked the narrow planks, handed the mugs to Steph on the front deck, then got down on all fours to turn around and crawl back to safety. She had forgotten the cat. She hadn't looked down into the water for fear of seeing the drowned remnants. She'd seen plenty as an orderly in the hospital, but this was different. She remembered that she had washed her hair in Cut water only the night before. She sat in the cabin to drink her cocoa, made up the fire and coaxed Candy to join her. It was clean and tidy, a miniature home, safe, comfortable, decent; a refuge from the weather, from past injustices, from present discomforts. She shared it with Steph, good-natured Steph; she'd have been miserable on her own. She sat comfortably; they'd call out if she was needed. Candy licked her hand and sat leaning against her comfortable legs.

Liz and Steph in the motor cabin kept their eyes away from the water. The fire was out, blankets on the side-bed still in a heap, plate and mug unwashed in the handbowl. But to Liz also it was a refuge, a home where she could live as she pleased, to please only herself. After tying up she could read until she slept; books were stacked in piles on the side-bed, second-hand books from the Caledonian Market which she scoured on the few days of leave they took after every third trip. She read anything, everything, preferred poetry, the moderns – Isherwood, Auden, Day Lewis, MacNeice – had made her own small contribution published in *Poetry London*.

She sat in the cleared space on the side-bed, swallowed the cooling cocoa in gulps, looked better. Steph sat on the step feet on the coal-box, shut her mind against the feel of the shaft in the sodden heap, hoped that the prop was free enough to turn.

"Ready for off?" she asked. Liz nodded. The engine would still be warm enough to start without Jan's help. It puffed on the second go, then cleared and resumed a welcome chug.

"Give a push and I'll try a few turns in reverse; might clear anything that's left." Instructions between them were minimal; they had worked together for long enough to know what was required. Steph stepped ashore, pushed off the stern with a careful foot and stepped back on the butty foredeck. She pulled in the loose length of snubber, carefully, praying that it would be free of kittens' remains. Washes from the blades, now turning gently, cleared the space between the boats; Liz had grimaced as Steph began to pull in the rope. The remains of sack on the bank were sufficient to convince them that little could still be round the prop. A burst from the motor in reverse, more black smoke, another burst as Liz put it hard ahead, and the smoke cleared. She eased the motor right down again; the length of snubber slowly unwound from the coils on the motor deck and then from the butty foredeck until Steph felt the lurch and once more they were under way.

Jan was at the butty tiller; Liz turned, gave the thumbs-up sign and Steph said a small prayer that they might make Tyseley without any further hindrance. Liz would ease through the bridge 'oles in neutral from now on – just in case! "Catherine de Barnes – Catty Carnes," she thought with a shudder, "shan't forget that in a hurry."

The rest of the trip was uneventful. Jan told Steph about the cat. Steph was fond of cats, called and called but there was no sight or sound of the spitting creature.

"Could have jumped back on shore again," said Jan, "before we got moving. Candy took a dim view."

"If not, he'll come out when we off-load. I'll put out some milk tonight on the cabin top, then we'll know. Cats like evaporated – it's like cream."

"Plenty of moggies at Tyseley to drink it if he doesn't." Jan didn't like wasting precious supplies on the rangy scavengers.

They wouldn't be off-loaded until the following day; plenty of time for shopping, baths, cinema, supper. They felt clean and civilized as they returned late to the boats tied singly along the quay ready for the morning. A thump in the cabin side at 7 a.m. was the usual signal that the grabs were ready; a reminder too that men were at work even though the women were still abed. There would follow a sudden lurch as the first load was lifted from the hold; teapots and mugs had been known to slide and shed their contents as the angle of the boat suddenly tilted. The 'girls' were old hands, had made the boats ready – sidecloths refurled and tied, the planks stacked on shore, cross-chains unscrewed, the holds open and ready for unloading – and they'd stay in bed whilst the lurching continued. Such luxury to lie there half awake whilst the men were working! They'd given up the cross-banter of self-defence, that their days started at 6 a.m., often continued through until 8 p.m. or even later when the evenings were light. They kept the cabin doors bolted; men weren't always respectful of their privacy. Liz would emerge when the motor hold was emptied to ensure that nothing else was lifted, to see the foreman, have a word with one of the men she recognized, generally to let them see that someone was about.

That first night they were garrulous and cheerful as they returned from the cinema, arms linked for companionship in the dark and silent yard. They took a last look round to see that all was ready for the possibility of an early start, let Candy out for a quick sniff and made for bed. Jan didn't envy Liz the isolation of the motor cabin; she was nervous when they tied in these desolate places, more so in the city than on an empty stretch in the country, although that was bad enough. '"Night," she said to Liz, "sooner you than me." They both laughed knowing what she meant. "See you in the morning," and Liz unpadlocked the cabin doors and disappeared down the black square of the hatchway.

Jan and Steph called to Candy and made their way to the butty cabin, to the familiar smell and feel of 'home'. They were stretched in their rough army blankets along the wooden side-bed and the bed cupboard, already drifting into the solid sleep of physical tiredness. "The cat," said Jan suddenly as the image of the dripping creature crossed her somnolent mind. "I didn't put out the milk." But Steph was asleep already and Jan soon drifted into forgetfulness, her last conscious thought, "The cat will have gone." Neither had told Liz about the cat not wishing to recall the wretched business of the kittens.

Liz was still awake. She could never sleep without first reading, however briefly.

> "Will you turn a deaf ear
> To what they said on the shore."

A temporary admirer had given her a volume of Auden's poems. The light flickered; damn, was the bulb going? She had forgotten to put new ones on her list. She half waited for the light to go:

> "For to be had for friend
> By an undeveloped mind . . ."

Again the flicker. She lifted herself on an elbow, listened. A scratching at the door – rats? They were used to rats, a scrabbling on the counter when they were held up at Maffas in the drought, a scraping and gnawing in the hold when they had carried grain to the Northampton Mills. Not rats, she decided, but a definite scratching at the closed cabin doors. A cat? What cat? Cats were

20

wary creatures, shunned strangers rather than sought attention. The scratching continued, urgent, demanding. Liz lit a candle. switched off the small light bulb. This was Birmingham, blacked out in fear of raids. Cautiously she lifted the bolt, pushed open one side and peered out. A cat it was; she could see it quite clearly in the half-light of the June night, sitting on the counter backed up against the ram's head. It glared at her, eyes glinting in the spiky, bedraggled fur. Cats! She'd had enough of cats for one day. "Clear off! Shoo!" she said, slammed the door shut again, blew out the candle and crawled down into the inter-folded blankets; warm, drifting . . . Scratch . . . scrape.

Blast the cat – the paint. "Clear off," she shouted. "Shoo – clear off." She fumbled for a plimsoll on the floor and threw it at the door; the scratching stopped; hopefully the cat had gone, taken fright, returned to its own haunts.

But Liz was now awake; her sleep was easily disturbed. She started to recite nursery rhymes to herself, an old trick which usually lulled her to sleep. "Baa, baa, black sheep, Have you any wool? . . . Pussy cat, pussy cat, where have you been?" The words took over from "Baa, baa, black sheep". Pussy cat, pussy cat; the torn sack of bloated corpses floated unbidden into her mind; nausea threatened. She turned on the light, she would not be sick. She sat up. She'd read some more, read until she fell asleep reading. The scratching started again; the faint crack of light must have drawn the creature back. Liz shivered, not entirely with the night's chill. Six months ago it had been the wailing and crying at Knowle – and now this . . . damn, damn, damn the cat – "all cats," she muttered. She filled the enamel jug with water from the kettle – precious tap water for the morning tea – flicked off the light, opened the door and threw the water at the wretched creature standing there with arched back, baleful eyes. It could hardly be wetter than it was already. Liz regretted her spiteful act immediately; the poor thing must have escaped a drowning in the Cut, was cold, hungry. She'd give it some milk. "Come on, then," she called more gently as it still didn't move. She found a bowl, poured in the evaporated milk and put it out on the counter. Still the cat made no move; Liz pushed the bowl nearer, she could smell the foul dankness of Cut water. She put out a hand to encourage the cat to drink; the white snarl at the side of its mouth seemed to lift as the cat spat and hissed, moved backwards onto the fender and tipcat. Suddenly it turned, leapt on shore and streaked away into the darkness of the wharf. Gone, thank goodness! She took up the untouched bowl, rebolted the doors, lit the small Valour stove, tipped the milk and the rest of the water into a pan, made a mug of cocoa which she drank in the warmth of the blankets and slept immediately, wakened only by the lurching of the boat.

Off-loading had begun. She hadn't even heard the banging on the cabin side. No water left in the kettle; she pulled dungarees on over pyjamas to refill from the water jug on the cabin top. A wet pool on the counter reminded her of the cat. She looked at the doors; no sign of any scratch marks. Must have stopped it in time, although the scratching had sounded quite fierce and had continued for a minute or so before she had emerged reluctantly from bed. However, the animal had gone; they'd be off again by midday and she had seen the last of it as it streaked away into the night.

The off-loading was finished long before midday, an easy cargo and the two men had frequent breaks. Liz made several brews of tea; one of them had given her a ¼-lb packet of Lyons – a generous gesture in days of rationing – and her gratitude overflowed into the almost continuous provision of mugs of tea while they worked regardless that her own meagre sugar ration was soon forfeited.

Steph and Jan emerged when work began on the butty.

"Should make the Black Boy – another early tie-up," said Steph.

"We'll join you for a pint," laughed the man slinging a cable round the bars. He was old enough to be their father, grizzled, paunchy, stained greasy trousers barely upheld by a thick leather belt. They chose to ignore his pleasantry; it was the man in the crane who had given them the tea.

Last-minute shopping, some fish and chips and they were off again, the empty boats breasted up and high out of the water. No wind to catch them so they should make good time. A brief interlude of leisure before the locks at Hatton and Knowle, all three of them together, Steph on the motor, Jan and Liz sitting on the sides of the butty well-deck. Not so clear and sunny as the previous day – lowering.

"Thunder about," said Jan.

"No wind, thank goodness." Liz hated the wind more than rain, more even than the frost. She remembered being forced to tie up for two whole days with the wind tearing through the empty holds making any move away from the bank impossible. Even the lighter winds, not strong enough to impede progress but gusty and unpredictable, made the work so much harder. "Wayward winds, wayward boats," she'd heard someone say; how true it was. Today was different, one which compensated for all the bad days. The boats looked well, cratches high, sterns into the water at just the right angle. "Nothing in the blades today," Liz silently prayed. "By the way," she remembered, "there was a cat on the motor counter last night. Wouldn't go away. Pretty wild it looked – wet too."

Jan looked at Steph and then told Liz of the cat which had fled for refuge when she rescued it from the Cut.

"Must have been the same one," said Liz. "Black – a white sneer on one side of its mouth. Poor thing! I threw a jug of water over it to frighten it off . . . it was wet enough already."

"Warm yesterday . . . you'd have thought it would have dried off by then."

"Perhaps it likes swimming," said Steph, who had been half listening. "Some cats do swim I've heard."

"I've never heard of a swimming cat." Jan was sceptical. "Couldn't have been the same cat. Moggies are two a penny round Brummagem."

The incident had already dimmed in Liz's mind. She started to sing 'As I was going to Strawberry Fair', with the other two joining lustily in the chorus. Another good-to-be-alive day; better than a classroom, better than a hospital ward. No one on the bridges out of Brum to spit, throw stones, yell inconsequential abuses. They were through the worst; there was Rowwood, a housing estate on the right, Heath Bridge, then a straight stretch to Catty Barnes – well over halfway to Knowle locks. At Knowle they'd see Noelle – spend a couple of hours there.

Catty Barnes Bridge was ahead. Steph had throttled down, memory of the sack reviving. Jan had gone below to make tea. Liz was perched on the butty gunwale enjoying the sultry warmth; she'd take over from Steph after the bridge. Candy was stretched on the cabin roof, luxuriating in the sun. How she hated the cold, wet days.

"A cat under the bridge," shouted Steph. "Looks wet and wretched," she added.

"God, not another cat," groaned Liz. "Speed up. We don't want it aboard."

Steph hadn't seen either cat – if two there had been – and was sorry for the poor bedraggled creature on the bank. She kept the speed steady.

"Poor puss, poor puss," she called.

"Shut up," shouted Liz. "Shut up. It's the same cat."

She leaned out to have a better look; it was the same cat she had seen during the night, she could swear it; spiky black fur still dripping with Cut water, glaring eyes – round and open even in the sunlight – a white snarl. It was standing at the coping, whippy tail upright, ears back, waiting for the boats. It opened a red mouth, silently; took a flying leap and landed on the cabin roof. Liz was terrified, unreasonably so, thought Steph. Then Candy yelped and dashed down into the motor cabin, whimpering and shivering. The cat stood at the end of the cabin, watching Liz, making no attempt to come nearer, water dripping from its sodden coat. Even Steph began to feel there was something odd about it. Jan looked out. "My god, it's the cat," she gasped. "The one I dragged out yesterday."

"Here, you take the tiller," said Steph to Liz, "I'll try to get it to eat – dry it off."

Liz stepped over reluctantly, eyes on the cat; it looked as if it could spring if she turned her back.

"Must have hidden in the hold after all. Goodness knows where though; thought I'd gone into every crack."

"The bunker," said Steph. "That's where it must have been." Jan pushed out a bowl of milk and Steph edged it towards the cat calling softly, if a little anxiously. It stood there, stiff, hard, staring, making no attempt to lick the wet fur, not even shivering. The only movement it made was to open its mouth several times as if to miaow, but without any sound. It refused to look at the milk although Steph pushed the bowl close with the end of the mop. The cat just moved sideways, ignored the bowl, continued to stare fixedly. Even Steph began to feel jittery.

"We'll never get rid of it," said Jan. "You can see it's determined to stay. Got a fix on us." She forced a laugh, but was clearly scared. Liz kept the chimney between herself and the staring cat.

Steph now pushed at the animal with the end of the mop. It never seemed to make contact; the cat moved each time to avoid the mop head, moved imperceptibly so that the mop head fetched up on the far edge of the cabin top. Even when she swept the mop in an arc the cat was able to avoid it almost without seeming to move.

They were rattled, each with the unspoken fear.

"Not natural," muttered Jan, who kept within the shelter of the cabin trying to reassure the wretched dog. Steph remembered the kittens. Liz stood stiffly behind the chimney for protection.

It stayed there until Barston Bridge; then, as they drew through the bridge it leapt for the shore as suddenly as it had come aboard. "It's in the water again," shouted Steph. Jan joined her in the well and together they watched the thin streak of the cat swimming back from where they had come. They watched until a bend hid it from sight.

"What do you make of that?" said Jan, but none of them felt disposed to put into words what each feared.

"It isn't natural," repeated Jan.

They made good time, tied up at the Black Boy, and went in later for drinks. It was a busy evening; a darts match, and they were invited to join in.

"Ever hear of a swimming cat around here?" Liz managed to ask the landlord, "Near Catty Barnes?"

The landlord laughed. "Good place to see one. Plenty of cats drowned up that way; sacks and stones you know. Not many escape even if they can swim."

There was no further opportunity for talk and the evening passed quickly and pleasantly, the cat temporarily forgotten.

Their trip continued, round to Longford Colliery for coal, back down to the Heinz factory to unload, down to Regent's Canal dock for re-loading – aluminium bars – and back again to Tyseley. They hadn't mentioned the cat episode; it was best forgotten. None wanted the others to think her superstitious. But as they worked up Knowle the image of the cat freshened in their minds. They had been held up at the top of Hatton while George, the fitter, looked out some spare coupling bolts. They had waited until he returned from a job; he was the only one to spare them such luxuries! So it was late afternoon before they reached

Knowle; it would be a late tie-up if they reached Tyseley.

"We'll go on a medium strap," said Liz at the top of the locks. "I'll take the motor. Steph, you on the butty. Jan, you make supper – and keep Candy with you." They both knew what was in her mind. Singled out, she'd be the first under the bridge at Catherine de Barnes; she didn't want to be separated from the others by the seventy-foot length of a towing snubber. "I'll come with you on the motor," offered Jan. "Your brass can do with some extra rubs. Only a tin of beans for supper anyway." Liz looked her thanks; she was scared; they all were.

Jan perched herself on the narrow width of gunwale, rubbed sporadically at the gleaming brasses. They hardly spoke, both tired, apprehensive as the bridges were passed. The road bridge was in sight – nothing.

"Nothing," said Jan. That was where the cat had disappeared. They looked ahead into the water; not a movement.

Henwood, Catty Barnes; they were just going through; not a sign of the cat on the coping or in the water. Liz turned briefly to wave her relief to Steph. At the same moment there was a light scraping thud and a gasp from Jan. The cat had jumped from the bridge above their heads, and landed again at the far end of the cabin roof; the same waterlogged cat with the white snarl at the side of its mouth. Liz screamed, backed away; nowhere to back except into the water, under the turning blades. Jan grabbed her belt as she put one foot on to the back fender. "Stop!" she yelled. "Stop, you'll be in." The boat began to swing and Jan pushed at the tiller, almost overbalanced herself as she still kept a hold on Liz's belt.

"Get it off, get it off," screamed Liz, hysteria rising. Jan, scared of the cat, scared of the turning blades and the swing of the bows for the further bank, managed somehow to turn the gear wheel into neutral, while the butty bows charged up alongside to push the motor further over into the mud. It had all happened in seconds.

"Get over to the butty," Jan shouted at Liz, tugging her back onto the counter. Somehow they scrambled over on to the butty and managed to join Steph in the comparative safety of the butty cabin. They abandoned the boats, shut themselves in, unmindful of the fact that the boats were left there to block the passage of any other pairs which might be travelling. They would leave the cat to its own devices, prayed that it would stay on the motor and leave them alone.

"It's still there," said Steph later when they had managed to calm Liz with strong sweet tea and aspirin. "Boats coming down." They had just appeared, empty boats breasted, back from Tyseley.

"I'm not going back until that cat has gone," said Liz.

"It's still there," repeated Steph, making no move to leave the security of the butty cabin. The cat was sitting now, silently glaring, still wet, bedraggled, pathetic. Pity overcame fear. The poor wretched creature was terrified, chased by dogs, children, harsh men with sticks, ruffians with stones, shouts, sacks, the Cut its only home, passing boats its only temporary refuge. Why their boats? Steph called again to the cat, "Puss, poor puss, come on, come here, puss . . . puss." The cat looked at her as if uncomprehending the soft, inviting tones, made no attempt to move. The oncoming pair drew nearer; they'd have to move out of the way.

"What are you doing?" called Liz. "Don't bring it over here. There's something wrong with it. Leave it alone."

"Boats coming . . . we'll have to go out . . . move the butty at least."

The cat's head turned; it had heard the oncoming boats above the steady thud of the still idling engine of *Hercules*. Suddenly it crouched, leapt onto the cratch of the butty, onto the towpath, streaked away up the side of the bridge and was gone.

"It's gone," said Steph. "Come on . . . I'll loose off the butty, pull it back out of the way. You two get the motor moving . . . hard astern back into the bridge 'ole." Steph was giving the orders; panic was now for the boats; the high bows loomed aggresssively.

"Think it's the Smiths," she shouted as the other two responded to the urgency in her voice.

"I'll pull back the butty. You take the motor," said Liz. Steph was the agile one; she ran along the top planks, over to the motor, threw off the towing strap and tossed it back over the butty cratch. Liz and Jan had got the butty moving, manoeuvred it clear of the bridge and back out of the way. Steph put the motor hard astern hoping to pull the boat back off the mud where it had drifted; luckily the butty had kept the stern back in the deeper water under the bridge. A few bursts astern and the boat came free – just in time.

"What's wrong? Want any help?" Charlie Smith had jumped off on to the towpath, leaving the tiller in charge of young Charlie who stood on a box enabling him to see over the cabin top.

"All right now," shouted Steph. "We caught a bag in the blades."

"Plenty of those around," said Charlie, 'catching' his boats as they slid past. "Watch out for bedsprings."

Jan and Liz waved to Charlie's missus as she looked out from the butty cabin. Jan was at the far end holding in the butty stern.

"Seen a cat?" she asked as the empty boats drew level.

"Lost one?" said Charlie.

"Found one. We don't want it – a stray, black, white . . . wet."

The boats were almost past.

"Sounds like the swimming cat . . . Catty Barnes . . ." shouted Charlie. They were almost out of earshot; Charlie did a pantomime putting an arm across his face as if to ward off a blow. "Take care . . ." his final shout just reached them. It did nothing to lessen their apprehension. There was the wait at Tyseley and the return trip.

For the present they saw no more of the cat, and reached Tyseley with no further incident. That evening they all three sat in the butty cabin delaying the time for bed. Steph had offered to sleep in the motor cabin, suggesting that Liz should move in with Jan. She was still more sorry for the cat than afraid of it; she thought she might even be able to help it, uncertain how, but believed that "love casts out fear" – although she would find it hard to persuade Candy who stayed firmly in her corner of the butty cabin.

"Sooner you than me," said Jan, "I'd not go near it for a million."

Liz: "Nor me. It's not a proper cat; I'm sure it isn't."

Steph: "What do you mean?"

Liz: "You know what I mean . . . it's not human . . . no, I mean it's not real."

Steph: "You mean we're hallucinating? We're not, you know."

Jan: "Charlie Smith says it's a swimming cat."

Liz: "*The* swimming cat . . . Catty Barnes . . ."

Steph: "Catherine de Barnes is the proper name – a woman, not a cat."

Liz: "Perhaps it was her cat – centuries ago, and it haunts the bridge where it once lived."

Jan: "Charlie also yelled 'Take care'. What do you think he meant?"

Liz: "What *I* think – that it's dangerous . . . evil. I'm still scared."

Steph: "Dangerous because *it*'s scared. Come on, let's be rational, either it's a real cat, homeless, terrified, hungry, has learned to swim from necessity, has a hideout somewhere around Catherine de Barnes; or else . . ."

Liz: "Or else? That's what I think."

Jan: "You really mean a ghost cat? That it isn't real? Somehow we see it but it isn't real?"

Steph: "That doesn't make much sense, does it?"

Liz: "But how did it appear here at Tyseley last trip? It's quite a trek from Catty B."

Steph: "Could have come on the boats. We thought at the time it could have hidden in the bunker. Remember?"

Jan: "I swear it wasn't aboard when we left. I really went through holds and bunkers."

Steph: "It just *could* have hidden – even in the engine-room. It's possible – all I can think of."

Liz: "Doesn't convince me. I agree with Jan – it's somehow a ghost cat – furious because of the kittens."

Steph: "That's rubbish. *We* didn't drown the kittens."

Liz: "No, but we released them – released the cat. It's out for revenge – revenge for all cats and kittens drowned in the Cut." Liz's imagination was flowing.

Jan: "But why us?"

Liz: "We were the ones passing at the time; we released the kittens and so we were kind of agents, the catharsis for the cat's grief and anger – the grief and anger of all drowned cats and kittens throughout the years. The cat we see is archetypal – a kind of image or prototype."

Liz wasn't too certain of the real meaning of the words recalled from old psychology lectures, but she convinced herself that she knew what she meant and Jan was certainly impressed. Steph remained sceptical. She had elected to sleep in the motor cabin and decided that they had talked enough.

"*I* don't believe in ghost cats, or catharsis, or prototypes," she said firmly. "I think it's a poor, lost, frightened moggy. Bed for me."

They spent two nights at the wharf waiting to be unloaded. Steph slept in the motor cabin undisturbed by any scratching.

"Didn't hear a sound," she replied cheerfully to their enquiries.

"You sleep too well," said Liz. "Nothing would wake you."

"Just as well. If I had heard it I'd have coaxed it in or fed it, but I didn't; it's still in hiding at Catty Barnes."

Finally they were off again southwards. Orders had come through that they were to return empty to the depot at Bull's Bridge. They hazarded a few guesses for the reason but weren't too interested. They were due for leave and they'd be spared the cleaning up after loading and off-loading coal. Should be an easy trip; sunbathing in one of the empty holds (weather permitting), washing on a line strung out along the length of the other – such luxuries! Catty Barnes and the strange cat were no longer mentioned. Leave and the prospect of a 'holiday trip', together with the warm June days revived their carefree, inconsequential moods of good-to-be-alive days. Liz sang, Jan polished, Steph dreamed and smiled. Liz would see Noelle again – the last time the baby had smiled and seemed to recognize her.

However, the return trip through 'Catty' had to be faced, the cat most likely would appear, for whatever reason.

"But it also disappears," said Jan prosaically. "We only have to put up with it for a couple of bridge'oles; half an hour at most. We'd best ignore it if it turns up."

"Agreed," said Liz. "Only I propose that Steph steers as she doesn't mind the cat, isn't scared. I *am*, and I'll be firmly down in the cabin if no one objects."

They didn't object. Liz did more than her share of the work most of the time; it was a small favour to ask. Jan wasn't sure; she was apprehensive, not panicky like Liz, but would take no chances. "I'll brew up as we go through," she volunteered.

They were off, laughing and planning what each would do on the leave ahead. Liz was staying in London with friends in Pimlico, hoped to see the film *Gone with the wind*, do some shopping and also to spend at least a day with Noelle.

"Home for me," said Jan. "Brother's home on leave, sick leave; has a friend staying for a few days, might be nice, you never know. Baths, dresses, dances. What'll you do, Steph?"

"Home too," said Steph. "Probably go walking, and baths, hair-do, sewing; could do with a summer dress."

So much they could do despite the continuing privations of clothing coupons, food rationing, travel restrictions, lack of money, lack of men, lack of opportunity to plan for a predictable future. However, now that the Americans were 'in', that Paris was freed and that the offensive had begun, there was the hope that the long years of war would end at last. What then?

"I shall apply for university and continue the fight to adopt Noelle," said Liz.

"I shall try again for nursing," said Jan.

"I don't know," said Steph.

The heath was on their right, the bridge in sight; the chatter stopped, eyes were stretched ahead.

"I'm going down," said Liz.

"Me too," added Jan. "You all right, Steph? I'll leave the door open. Shout if anything goes wrong."

What could go wrong? Steph expected the cat and there it was, ready to spring as the boat came level with the stone coping under the bridge. She would have been disappointed not to have seen it. The cat had landed much nearer this time, just beyond the hatch cover. If she stood in the hatchway, leaned over, she could touch it. The boats were through the bridge, no wind, on a straight course. She edged round the long tiller, wedged her back against the end of it and tentatively stretched out an arm.

"Puss, puss," she called softly, "come on . . . come."

The cat stood there motionless, eyes staring yellow slits in the snarling face, thin, wet fur streaked into its flanks, tense, waiting. Her hand moved to touch the creature; she smelled the clammy sodden dankness of the wet fur. Suddenly pain scorched through hand and arm. She screamed, drew back hand to mouth; blood. Jan was there, took the tiller.

"Get below." She pushed Steph over into the butty. "Get Liz to pour iodine on it – quick. Liz," she shouted.

"The cat," sobbed Steph, stumbling over into the butty. "The cat."

"It's gone," said Jan. And so it had. It streaked over the side and Jan saw it swimming, head and shoulders high as she had first seen it, back towards the bridge.

Suddenly Jan was in charge. "Let it bleed," she said as Liz looked up through the hatch to see if Jan was all right. "I'm OK. Look after Steph – tea. Use lots of iodine."

Liz disappeared. Jan took the boats to the top of Knowle, not a bump, not even a scrape through the bridges.

Steph and Liz appeared; the old tin teapot was filled several times. The smell of iodine pervaded; Steph dabbed sporadically but the bleeding had almost stopped.

"Tetanus," thought Jan. "You should see a doctor," she said. "Is it deep?"

"Not too bad," said Steph, stretching out her arm for inspection. The gash stretched from the back of her hand almost to the elbow, not deep but could be dangerous.

"We'll call at Sister Mary's on the way down," said Liz. "She'll cope if the iodine doesn't work."

Liz worked the locks, stiff heavy gates but with the pair breasted up it wasn't too bad. Jan's confidence and good judgement increased with each lock; she didn't even offer to let Liz take the motor and Liz in turn made no suggestion to take over. They tied at the bottom, just below the Black Boy, all tired emotionally as well as physically. The long scratch was re-examined; ten inches long, Liz measured. It looked clean, and was bleeding again. Jan found a tin of Germolene in her drawer, smeared some on a length of rag torn from a very thin pillow-case, covered the wound and bound it with further strips from the pillow-case.

"All in a good cause," she grinned, smug with her own success through the locks.

"What did you do?" she asked Steph. "Thought it liked you – if anyone."

"Put out my hand to coax it," Steph shuddered, remembering. "It was cold, wet, soggy; then it must have scratched me – frightened I guess."

"A maniac," said Liz. "Psychopathic if it was human. I don't think any cat could survive in the way we've seen it – always wet, hungry, demented. I think it's a reincarnation, caught in a time warp, forever doomed to live a wretched existence on the Catty Barnes stretch, trapped by its own misery and hate and spite."

Steph and Jan looked at each other, sceptical.

"You know, like the Flying Dutchman . . . but a cat. Why not?" added Liz with more assurance. *The Flying Dutchman*. In the film James Mason had been very convincing.

"The scratch is real enough," said Steph wryly. "It felt real enough, is real." Jan took a safety pin from her blouse to secure the makeshift bandage. Buttons get lost; Jan always kept safety pins for replacements.

"What's wrong with the arm?" asked George who had called in for a pint after finishing late at the yard. They told him.

"The cat again," commented George.

"You've heard about the cat before then?" asked Liz.

"Off and on," he replied. "Seems to favour some boats more than others. No one gets near it though – wild."

"How can it survive?" asked Steph. "Why the boats?"

"Well, there's tales of course, always is on the Cut. Could be it was chucked off a pair, left to fend for itself, wants to find its old home."

"But how long?" asked Liz. "How long has it been around?"

George looked at her. Girls were impressionable, easily off balance in his opinion.

"Some time," he said slowly over his beer and refused to be more specific. "Must be off; late already."

The landlord was a fairly recent licensee, hadn't heard anything of the cat. "Plenty of them around though. I suppose they keep down the rats," he said; his own plump and smug tabby was bunched comfortably on the counter.

"I'm tired," said Steph. Her arm felt stiff; supper, the drink – rum and orange as a 'special' – and the shock were having their effects. As they left the night air felt cold. June nights were unpredictable, warm and soft with summer scents, chill as with a premature sniff of autumn.

Two nights later they were at the top of Stoke. Steph's arm was still very stiff; she didn't seem too well, not much energy, was glad to lie in bed or sit in the well-deck nursing Candy, unlike her. Jan renewed the Germolene treatment and they all thought that the wound looked clean and healthy, was scabbing over.

Sister Mary's cottage was the mecca for all boat people and their ills. They tied there for her to deliver their babies; she strapped up broken limbs, tended and laid out the sick and the dead in the small confines of the boat cabins. She knew all the families, scolded the young, sympathized with the elderly – not so young herself. The surgery was the front room of her cottage, draped entirely in white sheeting; she herself was dressed in a nun-like habit of white with a white head veil. Liz and Steph knocked, were admitted and Steph's arm examined.

"Where'd you get this?" Sister Mary's voice was sharp.

Liz explained, omitting opinions and suppositions. "A cat," she said. "Wild, we think; it jumped aboard at Catherine de Barnes."

"Catty Barnes Bridge." It was a statement, not a question.

"How did you know? Have you heard of the cat before?" Liz asked quickly.

"Cats and cats," replied Sister Mary. "Plenty around." She drew back a sheet revealing a tray of surgical instruments.

"I'm going to open it – bleed and cauterize," she said firmly. "You should have had an injection. Foolish to have left it." She busied herself, ignoring Liz who was bursting with questions. She gave Steph a dose of whisky, then proceeded, removed the scab and squeezed the wound with forceps to encourage the blood flow, gave Steph another dose of whisky. Steph was definitely 'sozzled' thought Liz, and hoped that Sister Mary would offer her the same treatment.

"Reserved for patients only; better than anaesthetic." Sister Mary easily interpreted her look.

She lit a small methylated stove, then heated an iron. "Like half a pair of curling tongs," thought Liz. Steph had closed her eyes; it was Liz who shuddered at the smell of burnt flesh.

"Should be all right now; don't remove the bandage for a week. See me when you come back." She had smeared ointment on a thin strip of gauze and had renewed the bandage.

"What do we owe you?" asked Liz as she helped Steph down the steps.

"Put what you can in the box," replied Sister Mary. She indicated a shoe box with a slit in the lid on a small table by the door. "For the children," she said; they knew that she provided boots, socks, pullovers, and often food for the poorer boat people with large families.

Steph recovered enough to enjoy the rest of the trip although Liz and Jan did the boatwork. Later in life Steph was to make her home a refuge for stray cats. She inherited a small income when her parents died, gave up her work as a welfare officer, bought a cottage in Shropshire and, years later when Liz went to visit, there were more than forty cats in the cottage, in the greenhouse, in the dilapidated barn. The scar on her hand and arm still showed red and puckered. "Poor moggy," she said when Liz reminded her of the incident.

"I still don't think it was a real live cat," said Liz. "Thank goodness we never had to go through Catty Barnes again."

They had returned to Bull's Bridge, where they were asked if they'd prefer to work for Sam Barlowe on the Oxford run. The present pair was laid up as the crew, Christian, Stella and Jean, were leaving and S.B. wanted a replacement. No doubts; they accepted with alacrity. The Oxford run could be monotonous – coal to Osberton Radiators or to Wolvercote paper mills and empty back to the coalfields. But – single locks, tied up on Sunday (locks were padlocked through the summer), Banbury for shopping, the Oxford Rep., second-hand bookshops.

"And no more Catty Barnes," added Jan.

As it happened they only worked the boats for a further six months. The war ended, men began to drift back to the boats and the women left to live their separate lives, away from the Cut, from each other, from all the shared experiences of working, laughing, agonizing, talking, hating, even loving during those brief intense years as boatwomen trainees, on the Grand Union Canal.

Catty Barnes is now known as Catherine de Barnes. The swimming cat must have disappeared long ago, but maybe there have been others – abandoned, hungry, terrified – which wait for shelter on the passing boats; vicious cats, defensive and suspicious of the humans who are their enemies yet who provide the comfort, the warmth, the affection which attracts and repels them, which they cannot ignore, which they dare not trust.

Boats Coming

They left the Cut to live their separate lives, to pick up the frayed and tangled ends of their individual relationships, loves, occupations and interests which had been fractured, fragmented and cut short by the six years of war.

Opportunities materialized even as they had been abrogated.

Jan went to live in Barnet with her sister where she helped with the boys; their father had died at Dunkirk. She began to read, then enlisted at a local polytechnic for O-level courses. She had been impressed, despite herself, by Liz and Steph and what seemed to her the obvious advantages of a further education.

"You can do it if you really make up your mind," Steph had said; and Jan had plenty of determination. She took much longer than most to do the reading and write the essays, but had impressed the tutors by her application and the quality of improvement over the two years which it took to gain the required Os for acceptance as a probationary nurse. Her progress through the years was constant and, although the schedules of study and exams often stretched her to the limits of endurance, she never once regretted the efforts it cost. SRN, then ward sister, and finally assistant matron; that was all she wanted. Jan knew her own limitations; ambition was satisfied, she had achieved her goal. There had been a couple of men in her life, both patients. One had been married already and the other grew tired of waiting for Jan to 'finish'. He emigrated to Australia; sent her a card each Christmas.

Stephanie found it easy to get work; health visitors and social workers were much in demand. She had chosen Liverpool possibly with a barely acknowledged hope of meeting up again with Simon. She had attended a few political gatherings and made some enquiries, but there had been no sign or news of him. No doubt he had not survived. Men of his age group, his education and background were in short supply and she met no one in the course of the ensuing years to make marriage a possible alternative to the endless daily round of trying to ameliorate the insoluble social problems of the area.

She was over forty when she decided to devote her sympathy and resources to caring for homeless and unwanted cats. There had been so many of them in and around the derelict buildings in Bootle; sad, wary, scrawny travesties of the sleek and elegant pets she had known as a child. So often she was reminded of the Catty Barnes apparition by the same look of fear, mistrust, venom, interfused with a barely defined pathetic hope for security and warmth extinguished with the first tentative approach from a human. Her small basement flat was always home for several at a time, but most of the lodgers disappeared after sampling the few comforts she could offer. Two had remained constant, a scrawny, battered tabby and a small grey female. The two remained faithful to her and to each other – and there were always the kittens!

The cottage was not far from the canal at Audlem and Stephanie bought a small cruiser in which she took short holidays on the lovely stretches of the Shroppie, sometimes accompanied by Noelle, the adopted daughter of her old friend Liz.

Liz had married shortly after leaving the Cut. James was the brother of an old schoolfriend; a farmer, he had not been called up for fighting and was still unmarried at forty. Liz needed a home to meet with the conditions necessary for the adoption of Noelle. James had agreed reluctantly and after the marriage had ignored the child.

"Can hardly blame him," Stephanie had thought on her very infrequent visits (the cats were a good excuse). "Liz so obviously adores the child and it doesn't seem as if she and James are going to . . ." There was still time, though not too long as Liz had been thirty when they married.

The marriage had not lasted. There had been no children. Liz accepted a teaching post and two years later she applied for the deputy headship of a town school in the next county. She rented a couple of rooms for herself and Noelle and returned to the farm for weekends. The visits grew more infrequent; an ex-land army girl took up residence with James. There was no divorce or separation; both had agreed to go their own ways.

The years passed. Stephanie had grown stout with untidy hair; once blonde, it was now brown with barely discernible grey streaks. Jan changed little; capable and tidy in suits and twin-sets, her hands still strong and square with nails short and well cared for. Liz had aged more noticeably than the other two with a hard set to her mouth and eyes which seldom softened except in unguarded moments when she looked at Noelle. She had studied for a degree in psychology and took the post of lecturer in a teacher training college – in Liverpool – but Jan had left only the year before. Liz was restless still and even Noelle found her 'difficult'.

"Doesn't know what she wants," she had confided to Steph, and Steph had told her about those early days on the Cut and about the loss of Patrick and the baby.

"Why didn't she tell me?"

"She shuts it all away inside herself. Suppose it still hurts and always will. I don't know of any solution, Noelle."

"She's so efficient, too efficient. Sometimes it's like living with a computer."

"Well, you have Martin . . . she doesn't object to him?"

"She likes him, strangely enough. Thank goodness, or life would be impossible."

Noelle could dramatize as well as her mother, Steph had thought with a smile.

Those brief years of working and living on the Cut had left indelible impressions on all three. Separated widely in their life-styles, habits, opinions, interests and even widely separated geographically, the thread of the waterways insidiously twined its way through their relationships with each other – Jan, Steph, Liz and Noelle. They met sporadically, seldom all together, most often at Stephanie's cottage in later years.

Noelle was twenty-four, not unattractive but too thin, too taut, again like her mother. Her health was beginning to be threatened by the nervous and emotional demands made upon her by the work; she had been teaching for three years in one of the large comprehensive schools on the outskirts of Liverpool. Martin had gone, married to another teacher, younger than Noelle; she saw them occasionally and she still felt sad at his going; blamed herself. The nights were long and restless; she cried too easily and too often. An attack of shingles had necessitated a visit to the doctor, who advised Noelle that a break from teaching would be of more lasting benefit than the pills. Liz had been wonderful; she recognized the symptoms from which she herself had suffered in her own youth. As Noelle recovered but remained listless and apathetic, Liz tried to think of some way in which to stimulate and revive her daughter's spirits. She bought a small 'noddy' boat from Burscough on the Leeds/Liverpool canal, joined a local boat club and that summer they travelled up through Wigan, Blackburn, Burnley and Skipton in company with another small boat and its proud owners. They were a young couple – gay, cheerful and ordinary. It was their first long trip and they were glad to profit from the expertise of Liz and Noelle. They played cards in the evenings; Noelle joined them while Liz preferred to read and doze in their own boat. They offered Noelle a job in their small market garden.

"Can't pay you much," Les had said. "We've only just started. This is our honeymoon – last holiday we'll get for a few years."

Noelle resigned her teaching post and accepted Les' offer with enthusiasm. She put on weight, slept without the pills and joined a local choir.

In October a letter had come from Steph – the usual cryptic scrawl. News of the cats, the price of cat food, the latest litter and then, almost as a postscript: "Have been asked to do a trip down the old GU to take a boat from Farmers' Bridge down to Stoke. Belongs to a friend's friend. Son Giles is taking it – wants a mate – no one else available. Can Noelle come to look after the cats? Ten days at the most. Hope you're both coming for Christmas." A second letter (no phone at the cottage) gave a date – "late in November".

There was little work in the acre, nothing that Les couldn't manage, and he'd not have to pay Noelle's wages, although he offered. She thought that she might stay on with Steph until after Christmas and so it was agreed. Liz would join them as soon as possible.

The end of term came abruptly after the frenetic rush of marking, tutorials, lectures, writing reports, and coping with endless student demands. Liz was glad to escape. The cottage was warm and welcoming and Steph was genuinely pleased to see her. There followed days of talk, exchanges of news, introductions to additions in the cat families, and then there were the shopping expeditions and the preparations for Christmas.

Liz sank back in the sagging armchair. "What's wrong, Steph?" she asked on Christmas Eve over drinks. It was the day they kept for Noelle's birthday and they were all relaxed and warm by the open fire – cats everywhere. "You haven't even mentioned the trip. How did it go?"

"She hasn't said much to me either." Three cats were trying to edge each other from Noelle's lap. "Something happened, didn't it, Steph?" They both looked at her wondering why she didn't answer. Finally:

"You were always the one on the Cut to do the imagining, Liz. Jan and I were the sceptics about the baby crying at the top of Knowle – and then the cat at Tyseley. You always thought it wasn't a real cat, didn't you? I remember you talking about archetypes and some other such nonsense."

"*You* got the scratch. I suppose that was real enough, but it was odd how that cat just used to appear and disappear. Looked a bit like that kitten over there on its own."

"That's another rescue from the Cut," said Noelle. "Wish I could keep it. Found it at the top of Audlem locks."

Liz was still looking at Stephanie. "Come on, tell us about it. What happened?"

Stephanie took a long time in the telling, punctuated by questions, silences, more drinks, supper for themselves and the cats, and refuelling the fire. It was after midnight before she finished.

"Well, what do you think?" she asked finally. "Giles was as rattled as me," she added.

"It's a good tale," replied Liz. "God, how some of those boatmen could put the fear of the devil into one – never a good idea to cross any of them."

"Do you really think that some of those old boats are still on the Cut? Ghost ones I mean." Noelle had enjoyed the telling – a real ghost story for Christmas Eve.

"I don't know. I can only tell you what actually happened."

"I wonder if anyone else has heard – or seen 'fly Charlie'." Noelle poked up the dying fire then looked at her mother. "You ought to write that story, publish it and then someone might read it, someone who's also met up with this character who gave Steph and Giles such a fright."

"No time," said Liz defensively.

"The next three weeks," said Noelle. "Shouldn't take you that long. Steph's given you all the info."

Steph was also looking at her somewhat quizzically. "You always wanted to write, didn't you? Now's your chance."

There was no escape. Noelle gave her an early New Year's present of a dozen biros and Stephanie found a pile of typing paper left over from the days of writing reports. Liz started reluctantly but, as she wrote, the story took shape. She read out her efforts to the other two; they were good listeners and were glad that Liz, for once, was less fidgety and restive than usual.

The story was written, approved of and put away with other written and partly written articles which Liz had never found time or energy enough to follow through. She wrote the story in the first person as if Steph herself had written it. After all, it was her story.

The following Christmas they were again with Steph, and Noelle asked Liz to take the story for a Christmas Eve read by the fire.

"Sentimental nonsense," Liz had laughed, but she picked out

the manuscript from all the other agglomeration of papers with a speculative gleam in her eye.

"It was late November," she read, as the three of them sat over the fire as they had done the previous year . . .

It was late November and I set out for New Street Station; pullovers, socks, gloves, and change of underwear packed into my well-worn – somewhat outdated – rucksack. How I coveted the newer variety – nylon on a serviceable frame, light and strong. My own was grey canvas, cumbersome, still smelling of damp and mould from its long hibernation in the cottage cellar. I felt apprehensive, slightly ridiculous; a middle-aged woman – late middle age – with a rucksack, dressed in jeans and anorak. Even more ridiculous my fellow travellers would think me if they knew that I was off to join a young man on a boat; this time of the year, too. I hoped that the young man, Giles, would be at the station to meet me; the rucksack was quite heavy.

I knew Giles quite well; his Aunt Myra was an old school-friend of mine and she had frequently brought him to the cottage to talk about the boats. He was moonstruck about the canals; used to borrow the noddy and in return kept it in good repair – suited us both. I had a sneaking hope that he and Noelle might get together; never said a word to Liz but think she guessed. They were good friends, enjoyed the boating . . . I was still thinking about the two of them when the train drew into New Street. Giles was there, bless him; good, reliable young man. He was in the Merchant Navy, seemed to have a lot of time ashore and this leave he had promised to take the *Alphons* from Farmers' Bridge down to Stoke Hammond for friends of his aunt. I believe they were worried about the vandals in the Brummagem basin and wanted the boat nearer to London where they lived. Giles – bless him – asked me along for the trip, just a few days. Noelle offered to come and feed the cats and I took Sandy along with me. Sandy was my latest 'rescue' and was terrified of the other cats and only seemed to relax when he came aboard the *Karianne* with me. I guessed he had been used to a boat and somehow had strayed or been left behind.

"Hey there, Steph." Giles had seen me before I saw him; he seized my rucksack and made a way through the crowds while I followed with Sandy in his basket.

"Mind walking?" he asked. Of course I didn't; a good stretch after sitting in the stuffy carriage was welcome.

"A cat as usual, I see. Which one this time?"

"Sandy," I panted, trying to match his long strides.

We settled in. The *Alphons* was pure luxury; an almost new boat beautifully lined with the red-gold of pirana pine. I noted with joy the central heating from a Torglow stove in the saloon.

"Two sacks of phurnacite on board," said Giles, "so we'll keep warm. Water tanks are full and plenty of diesel. A nice cosy trip." He'd been on board for the past two days, and had bought provisions and made all the necessary preparations.

"Lovely, lovely boat," I said. "Tell me more, Giles. Who are the lucky owners?"

"An elderly couple who live in Hackney. They're interior decorators who have made a pile and hope to retire at Christmas. They intend to live aboard. Lucky devils."

"You met them?"

"Aunt Myra phoned mum. Lucky I was due to come home on leave; so I went over to see them. Nice old boy – fiftyish, energetic, crazy on the canals. He had the *Alphons* built to his own design."

"Has an eye for comfort," I said, noting the plush Axminster carpeting.

"No expense spared he said. Good engine, too. And a proper boatman's cabin. I'm sleeping round there. I like to look out at the stars."

"Warm enough?" I asked.

"Come and see," and we sat in the small back cabin with the doors open on to the water and the cold November afternoon. There was a lovely iron stove smouldering away and the heat was terrific; quite like old times but so much more comfortable.

My own cabin was the last word in luxury; even a sprung mattress. And there was a real bathroom. I was going to enjoy this trip.

"Ready for off in the morning?" Giles asked over tea.

"Just hope I'll wake up; that bed looks the last word in comfort."

"The engine will soon get you going. But we don't have to hurry. Nine o'clock all right? Feel up to the locks, or would you sooner steer?" he asked.

"Locks," I said hurriedly. "I'll do the locks. The beautiful paintwork scares me to death; I'd be sure to scrape it against the sides."

The next day was dull and misty but it was exciting to think of being on the move again. Giles was a competent boatman and after the locks I'd be able to settle and enjoy being aboard such a super boat. The day was a dream; hardly any other boats on the Cut. Sandy had settled in as if it were home from home and staked his claim to a stool by the warmth of the fire. A real locking day, so that by the time we had gone through Farmers 13 and Ashted 6 we both felt well back into the routine. Camphill, Knowle, Hatton – forty more locks; it wouldn't exactly be a leisurely few days although there was no pressure to keep going as in the old days. We could stop when we felt tired and the pubs along the route were now plentiful and comfortable; we'd make the most of what they had to offer.

Three of the few boats which we met were working up through the Hatton flight of twenty-one locks so that we sailed down with little effort. We tied up at the Cape, an old familiar pub from wartime days of working; we intended to make an early start the next morning. The days were short and by 4 p.m. it was necessary to be on the look-out for a mooring.

Unfortunately (for us!) the cider at the Cape is rather potent and, with the warmth from the fire and in the company of a friendly darts team from Warwick, we drank far more than we intended. We had also been persuaded to make up the locals' side and it was well after midnight before we staggered out into the night air. I think our team had won and several returned with us to the boat for further celebrations.

It was almost midday before we finally surfaced and got under way. As it was already late we decided to have an easy day and to make for the Blue Lias at Long Itchington. I think we had also arranged to meet the Warwick team there, but that was completely forgotten in the events which overtook us before we could reach the warmth and security of the pub.

We pounded along uneventfully through Leamington and Radford and then picked up something on the blades under the railway bridge. It took the best part of an hour to free them and the shaft from the offending wire and length of rope. It would be dark now before we reached the Blue Lias but, with luck, we still ought to make it before opening time.

The spread of locks up to Bascote 4 stretched ahead and I decided that a walk would help to clear my head, and also I would save a little time at each lock by opening a gate ready for the boat to enter. Uphill locks, I thought, so they should be empty. It's a lovely stretch of country and the towpath makes for good walking. The Fosse locks were almost empty and to lift a paddle and open the nearside gate was the work of seconds. I sat on the beam to watch the *Alphons* approach; with both chimneys smoking it spelt home and comfort on that bleak, wintry afternoon. There wasn't a sound except for the dry brush of reeds in an occasional sigh of the wind.

It's a longish stretch to Wood Lock and Giles suggested that I should come aboard, but I was enjoying my walk and thought I'd have time to brew up tea in the stretch before Bascote; it would taste better for having to wait a little longer. Giles was prodding away at the propeller from the lock side, wrestling with still more wire, so I set off to get well ahead before the boat got under way. It would be dark early with no moon until much later. The ground was hard – not much rain lately – and a slight mist hung above the reeds on the far bank. The spinney trees stood gauntly and I was reminded of a line from Keats: "The sedge is withered from the lake and no birds sing." The words seemed appropriate somehow. I looked back; the *Alphons* wasn't in sight. Giles must be still untangling the wire; I half-wished I had stayed aboard to brew up in the cosy warmth of the cabin. I hoped he wouldn't be too long.

However, the lock was in sight and someone was sitting on the balance beam. A boat coming, I wondered, or was it just a hiker or perhaps a workman on his way home? As I approached I could make out the humped back of what surely must be a boatman, but in the uncertain light I couldn't be sure. My heart jumped a bit; I hoped it *was* a boatman and not some disturbed psychopath mooning around. The loneliness of the place on a cold winter afternoon was somewhat chilling and I strained my ears for the homely sound of an oncoming boat. Nothing from either direction. I glanced back along the straight but there was still no sign of the *Alphons*. Idiot, I thought tensely, why the hell doesn't he come?

The figure on the beam didn't move and had his back to me, hadn't heard me probably. I now saw that the lock was full and that both top gates were open. Good, I thought reassured, there must be boats coming; working boats I hoped. There were too few of them these days and it was such a joy to see them slide so easily alongside into the lock and to watch the speed and skill of the crew who operated them. There were times when I forgot the hardships and longed once again to experience the thrill of achievement in working with a pair of loaded boats up the stretches from Limehouse to Tyseley Wharf. It could be that I would recognize the boats and the crew as they came into the lock. I took the windlass from my belt to indicate that I too was a boater. I walked to the lock side. Still no movement from the man sitting there. Now I could see clearly the shape of his windlass crooked into the small of his back, the sweat rag round his neck and the slouched hat pulled low so that his face was almost hidden. His arms were folded, hands hunched into his armpits, to keep them warm most likely. I looked sideways at him.

"Boats coming?" I asked.

No answer.

I strained my ears for the sound of an engine. Nothing. The absolute silence was unbroken and even the rustles of wind in the reeds had died. I felt uneasy; there was, however, nothing for it but to wait so I perched on the old wooden bollard at the lock side.

I felt rather than saw the boatman move his head slightly as if to look at me. Reassured, I turned more fully to look at him. It was hard to make out any detail in the gloom but I could just see a stubbly chin and had the impression that he was an oldish man, although it is difficult to tell with boat people. I took courage again.

"Your boats left Welsh lock yet?" I asked.

He didn't answer and a prickle of apprehension crept up the back of my neck. He might not be a proper boatman; perhaps he was an eccentric who lived in a fantasy world of boats and dressed up for the part. There were such characters, Walter Mittys who lived nostalgically in a bygone age when boats and canals were viable commercial propositions. Harmless anyway, I thought hopefully, and he really didn't look very big. Boatmen were usually small and wiry although strong, I remembered apprehensively, as even the skinniest could wind up a paddle while I was still taking my first turn.

I felt that I must talk to break through this chill of silence.

"Which are your boats?" I asked. "What are they called?"

To my relief a gasping wheeze came from the hat. He cleared his throat several times as if it were clogged with dust – coal dust most likely. Then he spat expertly into the lock.

"*Orris* and *Hecooba*," he croaked.

"*Horace*?" I asked again.

"And *Hecooba*," he repeated and got up from his perch. The names of the boats sounded vaguely familiar, but no more than that. He stood by the lock side, small and a good six inches shorter than I, although he lost a few inches through his stoop.

"What are you carrying?" I asked, to keep the conversation going. Another silence and I found myself straining for a sound of boats – any boats from either direction. Finally —

"Bars," he said gratingly, "Aluminium bars fer Brummagem . . . Tyseley," he added.

It sounded strange. Tyseley Wharf hadn't been used in years; but perhaps this was a special scheme to revive the commercial traffic again; or perhaps a film was to be made . . . perhaps . . . I wanted to ask more but he had taken out his windlass and had slouched over to the top end of the lock.

Now, at last, I heard the faint chugging of the *Alphons* engine and saw the welcome shape in the distance. What a relief. I ran back down the towpath to warn Giles that boats were coming down and the lock was against us.

"Boats coming," I yelled as he approached. "*Horace* and *Hecuba*."

"Working boats?" he shouted in reply. "*Horace* and *Hecuba*? Never heard of them." That wasn't surprising, although Giles reckoned that he knew all the boats working on the Grand Union. He and his parents were real enthusiasts.

"Nor me – but the lockwheeler's holding the lock."

"Hope they won't be long," said Giles going astern to halt the speed of the *Alphons*. "Getting dark already."

I thought the other boats couldn't possibly be much longer. I had been at the lock for at least ten minutes, probably more, and boatmen didn't usually send lockwheelers on so far ahead. He should have got off at Longhole in which case the boats would have been through and past us long ago. Even if the lockwheeler had walked from Welsh Lock, which now seemed likely, the

boats still should have arrived at the lock. It was decidedly odd.

"Anything wrong?" shouted Giles.

"Not sure," I said, keeping close to the stern of the boat as it edged forwards. "But there's no sign of his boats and he had the lock ready when I arrived."

"Go and ask him to let us through. We'll only be ten minutes at the outside."

I felt panicky at the suggestion. "I'm freezing," I excused myself. "Let me on and you go and ask him."

Indeed I was freezing. I had grown cold with hanging around and the cold had shrivelled up my courage. I didn't much fancy asking a favour from the surly boatman; probably he'd respond better to another man. Giles edged the bows towards the bank. Mud . . . and the bows were still a good five feet off. Giles could have jumped off but no way could I have got on.

"Where is he?" said Giles. "Tell him I asked to go through."

"He's still up at the top gates." I could just make out the shape of him leaning against the paddle support. "OK, I'll go and ask – he can only refuse. You go astern for entering."

I could sense the man watching us as we talked, and doubtless he could hear every word in that cold stillness. I was being stupid; any boatman would let us through if his own boats were delayed, which must have happened to the *Horace* and *Hecuba*. I gripped the handle of my windlass more tightly and swung it to keep up my courage. I'm not usually nervous but as I approached the lock once again I felt the sweat trickling round my armpits and my one instinct was to race back down the towpath and to clamber aboard even if I had to wade. I looked back and saw the *Alphons* going astern to the far side of the Cut. Escape was impossible and, somehow, I forced myself back up to the lock.

The boatman was still by the open top gates and, as I approached, started to swing his windlass – a swivel brass-handled windlass I saw. He looked more business-like – 'life-like' I almost said – swinging his iron as I had been doing back on the path. I had tucked mine back into my belt to leave my hands free for closing the gates. There was still no sign or sound of approaching boats.

"Can you let us through?" I asked in what I hoped was a persuasive voice. "We'll not take long and your boats seem to have been held up."

He didn't answer but kept on swinging his iron as he turned his back to face away from me. I was determined now to empty the lock; his gesture and his refusal to answer had both insulted and angered me – I'd show him! I crossed over the bottom gates. After all, I was a good hefty female and he looked but a pinched-up, skinny little man and I knew that I too could swing a windlass to good effect if necessary. I moved deliberately up the side of the lock; I could feel his eyes upon me from under the pulled-down hat although he still kept half-turned from me. I ignored him and started to pull on the gate. It began to move and the result upon the boatman was terrifying. He turned, swinging his windlass wildly above his head and threatened me across the width of the lock.

"Boats coming," he cackled. "Boats coming. Leave 'er be."

"They're nowhere near. We've waited long enough. I can't even hear them . . . and we're ready to go through," I shouted firmly, determined to be polite no longer. Action had given a slight edge to my courage and I now succeeded in closing the gate. I decided to draw up the paddle on one of the bottom gates for a few notches to ensure that the gate stayed closed and also to facilitate the closure of the other gate where the boatman was still threatening me. I then crossed over and raced to pull on the balance beam. I kept my windlass in my hand ready for action if he tried to stop me; as I pulled I half expected to be attacked. I was scared, but also determined that this wretched little man wasn't going to stop me. The gate was heavy but began to swing easily with the flow of water and I had to move quickly to avoid losing my balance. The boatman had gone; and then I heard the ominous sound of a paddle being dropped. The gate closed with a bang. I saw him run up the lockside opposite and begin to pull open the gate I had first closed. I was mad.

"Let the bloody thing alone, will you!" I yelled. "We're going through and you'll not stop us." Fatal words . . .

He faced me across the lock. "Open up . . . boats coming, boats coming . . . boats coming," he repeated, still threatening. I almost gave up but then Giles' voice broke through from the dark stretch below the lock. "Hurry up, I'm on the mud. Anything wrong?"

"OK. Shan't be long," I shouted back more hopefully than I felt. Perhaps the sound of Giles' voice would halt the wretched

51

boatman; he'd think twice about attacking me if there was a man aboard the waiting boat.

I was determined to empty the lock, to raise a paddle and to close again the gate which he had almost opened. I took a couple of turns and looked to see if the gate was closing. To my horror the boatman, realizing that he could not hold the gate open against the flow of water, came for me down the lock side whirling his windlass ready for action. I didn't stop to think how large and tough I was; this was a demon brandishing a lethal weapon and I was terrified. I crashed down the side of the lock forcing my way through brambles and rushes, desperate to reach the safety of the boat. My feet sank into the mud as I shouted hysterically to Giles for help. I felt pursued by venom and hate, waves of it overtook me as I stumbled on through the reeds until I was half lying in the water, my feet submerged in the sucking mud. Giles had seen my panic and heard the urgency of my shrieks for help. I felt the long shore plank being levered under my outstretched arms. I clutched it desperately and somehow managed to pull myself clear of the mud.

"Clear off you sod," yelled Giles. Later he told me that he could see no one but he thought he'd let the bugger know there was a man aboard. The sound of his voice helped to calm my hysterical fear and I was able to wriggle my way along the gang plank. Giles clutched me and finally I was back on board, covered with mud, scratched and bleeding and shivering uncontrollably.

"He'll kill me . . . he'll kill me . . . he's mad . . . evil," I heard myself saying over and over. Giles got out the brandy bottle and I swallowed all he gave me. It was light and warm in the cabin and Sandy, the cat I had taken for the trip, was asleep on the stool; it all looked so normal and comfortable. I was making great muddy pools on the carpet.

"What the devil happened?" asked Giles as I calmed down and was able to talk more coherently. I was still shaking as I told him. I felt thankful that we were marooned in the middle of the Cut and inaccessible to that lunatic boatman out there.

It was Giles' turn to be mad. Despite all I could say he was determined that a crazy boatman wasn't going to hold us there all night in the middle of nowhere.

"Don't worry, I'll deal with him," he said. After all, Giles was six feet tall and tough; I couldn't believe that the mad boatman would threaten him or prevent him from using the lock. I was only a woman and no boatman considered a woman, any woman, to be a threat. He'd be rather more wary of a tough looking young man who meant business.

Giles edged the bows back towards the towpath and slid the shore plank across the remaining gap. I stood shivering on the counter ready to straighten up the boat and to enter the lock directly the gates were opened. Giles pulled the plank onto the bank to save me from having to leave the counter. I switched on the headlight and turned the bows so that the light would pick out the gates and the top rails. The stars were beginning to show. A frost, I thought, and took another swig of the brandy. My ears were strained to catch any sound of words but I could hear nothing. Then Giles leaned over the top rail.

"No one here," he shouted. "Must have given up and gone to find his boats. Shan't be long now. Top gates are still closed." A wave of relief flowed through my brandy-lined stomach.

We'd stop below Bascote rather than work up through in the dark. Then I thought that we'd be sure to meet up with *Horace* and *Hecuba* and it looked now as if they must be tied up at Bascote. I had no wish to be tied up anywhere near that fierce little boatman, so it would mean that we'd have to keep going to get clear of them. The possibilities of meeting them or not meeting them skipped through my mind as I watched Giles cross the gate to wind the further paddle. I put the engine in astern, straightened up the boat with the aid of the short shaft and then put her slightly ahead to counteract the flow of water. Suddenly, through the soft thudding of the engine there was a rattle and a clang and the flow of water ceased abruptly.

"Catch must have slipped," I thought. Giles was bending over the paddle gear on the towpath side; he'd be making sure the catch on that side was in position. I could see him in the light from the headlamp wind up the paddle, check the catch again and then cross the gates to rewind the first paddle. He had just reached the far side when again there was a fierce rattling as the second paddle fell hurtling back into position.

"Careless clot," I thought crossly and heartily wished we could get clear of the wretched place. I still expected to see that bent little figure racing along the lock and coming at Giles with his windlass.

"What's the matter with the catches?" I yelled. I had put the engine into neutral and clambered along the roof to have a better look at what was happening. Giles was examining the catch of the first paddle.

"All right as far as I can see," he shouted. "Can't think why it slipped off. I'll have another go."

He wound each of those paddles four times. I counted mechanically in the cold frozen fear of realization that he'd never succeed in lifting the paddles to empty the lock. Boats were coming weren't they? Each time that he crossed the gates the paddle he had just wound up dropped back into position of its own accord. I knew that the boatman was there, and I knew just what he was doing although in the growing darkness I was not certain that I could actually see him. He was able to skip with incredible agility across and round the lock always keeping out of range and out of sight from both Giles and myself. But he was there all the same, I knew; and he intended to hold the lock for his boats, wherever they were.

"Come back," I finally managed to shout. "He'll never let us through." I put the bows hard into the bank on the towpath side. "Get the plank across and come aboard," I yelled, but Giles was already down on the bank trying to manoeuvre the plank into position. I edged along the gunwale to grab the end when it came within reach and made for the comparative safety of the well-deck. By leaning right over the side I was just able to grasp the end, but it was heavy and slippery with mud and I dropped it back into the water, unable to lift it back onto the side of the boat.

"Throw a rope," shouted Giles as the bows began to drift back from the mud. I thought I could see the boatman watching us from the top of the lock, but in the dark I couldn't be sure. Giles said later that he caught glimpses but that each time he turned to face him the boatman vanished. In the shadows of the lock, shapes materialize and vanish like tricks of the imagination and neither of us was certain that he was still there as we wrestled with the shore plank. But the drop of the paddles was no imaginary trick; they stayed down and would stay down however many times Giles would wind them up.

Finally we managed to get the plank across to the bows and Giles came aboard and pulled the plank in after him.

"Where's the brandy?" he asked.

We backed off from that devilish lock and sat in the middle of the Cut well away from the dark menacing shape of the gates. It was so quiet; the boat made no movement in the stillness of the water. Neither of us mentioned the possibility that boats would be coming through; we felt isolated in some strange happening that wasn't over yet. The Blue Lias seemed a thousand miles away. We could have gone ashore and walked there but neither of us even suggested that we should make the effort. I was too tired and too terrified to move from the island of light and safety that was our cabin and Giles made no effort to go outside once we had drawn the curtains and closed the doors.

We finished off the brandy and got out the cards. It was still quite early, only about 8 p.m.

"I'm starving," said Giles, and I realized that we hadn't eaten since we had swallowed meagre slices of toast as we left the Cape; hours and hours ago that seemed. I cooked an omelette and made a great jug of coffee. We didn't mention the paddles, although with every slight sound we both looked at each other, listening. It isn't over yet, I thought, trying to force mouthfuls of omelette into my reluctant stomach. Afterwards we played bezique, but my mind wasn't really on the game and I missed most of the points.

"No good," said Giles. "We might as well get some sleep. I'll doss down in here tonight." He usually slept in the boatman's cabin at the stern of the boat, and that meant going outside as there was no way through to the boatman's cabin from the main cabin. Neither of us felt inclined to go outside.

Sandy stretched and walked over to the doors.

"Blast the cat," I said. "I'd forgotten him. He probably wants to go ashore."

"Well he can't, can he?" said Giles. "I'm not getting that plank across again."

I was just thinking that I'd have to put the cat litter out for him when I remembered that it was stored in the engine-room. Suddenly he bristled all over and with a loud 'wow' shot up onto the top of the piano. He sat there, eyes wide, fur on end, staring at the door.

"What is it?" I whispered, almost choked with the thumping of my heart. Giles lurched towards the doors and flung them open. The cratch cover was over and pinned down against the night. He flicked on the light in the well-deck; nothing there – but Sandy was still crouched low on the piano top, growling.

"Nothing," said Giles. He closed the doors again and gradually Sandy relaxed, although he made no further attempt to go out.

"Cat litter's in the engine-room," I said. "If he messes, it doesn't matter. I'd rather clean up in the morning than go out there."

We both of us felt that we were waiting. I suppose that we *were* waiting – waiting for those damned boats to come down through the lock. We forced ourselves to play two games of cribbage and by 11 p.m. we packed up for bed. I decided to sleep in the small cabin just the other side of the galley bulkhead and Giles used the sleeping-bag kept under the saloon couch. I was tired now; the effects of all the brandy, the walking and my frantic efforts to escape the boatman had me yawning and ready for bed. I fell asleep almost immediately.

I have no idea how long I slept. I slept . . . and then I was completely awake almost knowing what must happen. I wanted to call Giles but every part of me except my hearing seemed paralysed. We had left one of the cabin lights on, but I could see nothing, nothing but that bent little figure winding away at the paddles. I could only listen and follow in my mind every move of those boats coming down through the lock. There was a slow rush of water and I could feel the *Alphons* move slowly astern and then sideways into the reeds. As the rush of water eased I heard the familiar phut-phut of a Bolinder engine. It grew clearer and I could imagine the great gates swing slowly inwards. There was the rattle I had been expecting, the rattle of paddles being lowered as the first boat left the lock. In my mind I could follow every move as the motor boat went ahead and then eased back into neutral as the steerer – who was he? – bent to pick up the butty strap – a fairly short strap I thought. My brain was working like clockwork whilst my body lay stiff and rigid under the quilt. Was Giles awake? I couldn't call and there was no sound from the saloon. All I could do was to listen and to wait for the boats to come nearer and nearer. *Could* they pass or had the *Alphons* blocked the narrow channel? The Bolinder eased right down and I knew that the bows were drawing level. The beam of the head-light moved along the drawn curtains; it kept going. I could feel the boat passing – passing, thank God; but there was still the butty to follow. The bows of the *Alphons* must have swung out in the slight wash from the motor.

"Keep over can't you – boats coming – keep over." I heard that harsh grating voice which struck fear right through to the very marrow of my being.

There was a good nudge as the bows of our boat hit the butty and then scraped along the butty side. Our side doors were on the offside or I was sure that the boatman would have come hurtling into the cabin ready to swing at me with his windlass. I held my breath as the Bolinder's revs increased and the butty was pulled away. It had almost passed when I heard a crash at the back end of our boat. The chimney – he's bashed the chimney on the boatman's cabin with his windlass and knocked it off. I remember hoping that the chain would hold.

"What's happening? You all right? Thought I heard some-thing." Giles was awake. Relief flowed through me like the warmth of the brandy. I crawled out into the saloon where Giles was sitting half-cocooned in the sleeping-bag. He was still not very awake but was listening; the crash had probably woken him.

"What's wrong? Have I missed something?" he mumbled.

"Didn't you hear? They went by."

"Didn't hear a thing. Sure you weren't dreaming?" A look at my face assured him that I was not. I made up the fire and spent the rest of that endless night in the chair although I knew there was nothing else to wait for. The boats had come and they were through the lock and off up to Tyseley. Giles wriggled free and peered out through the cratch cover.

"Nothing," he said, "but we're well over into the reeds and on the mud." He heated up the rest of the coffee and was soon back into the warmth of the sleeping-bag. I suppose that we both must have snoozed the rest of the night away.

In the cold morning light the lock was empty and the bottom gates were open, ready for us to go through. I looked out at the bows and the fender had been dragged to one side as if caught by an oncoming boat.

"Look at the chimney on the boatman's cabin," I said to Giles as he went to start the engine.

"It's still here," he called, "but hanging over the side. Lucky the chain held."

No wind, no trees; how else could the chimney have become dislodged from the tight fit of the collar?

We tied up at the Blue Lias and went in for a midday drink.

"Any boats about?" Giles asked the landlord.

"Nothing," he replied. "The Cut is dead at this time of the year. You're the first boat we've seen for a couple of days."

"What about the *Horace* and the *Hecuba*," I asked as casually as I knew how. "Didn't they go by last evening?"

The landlord slowly put down the glass he had been wiping. "What do you know about the *Horace* and the *Hecuba*?" he asked.

Between us we told him the events of the past evening. He listened without interruption but poured himself a very large whisky.

"Well, what do you know about the boats?" I asked impatiently while he thoughtfully finished his drink.

He didn't answer directly.

"Hey there, Alec," he called across the room to one of the BWB workmen off the dredger. "Come over here, will you, and tell these folks about the *Horace* and the *Hecuba*."

The effect upon Alec was startling. We had barely noticed him talking and drinking with several others in a darker corner of the room. There was a silence as he stood and detached himself from his mates. He was short and bent and as he came towards us I gripped the counter for support; it was as if the old boatman was standing there fixing me with the malevolent stare.

"What d'you know about them boats?" he asked in the same harshly grating voice.

"They went through Wood Lock last night," said Giles. "The old boatman stopped us from coming through – said he had to hold the lock for his boats and dropped the paddles as soon as I wound them up."

A cackle of laughter seized Alec and his sharp ferrety eyes disappeared into the wrinkles and creases of his face.

"It wasn't so funny at the time," I said sharply. My courage had soon returned under the interested scrutiny of several pairs of eyes.

"That's old 'fly Charlie' all right," he said. "Lucky fer you he didn't scalp you with that iron of his. You wouldn't have been the first."

"What exactly do you mean?" asked Giles. "Who's 'fly Charlie' and what about those boats that no one else seems to have seen?"

"What'll you drink?" the landlord asked Alec, giving Giles the wink. Giles was quick to respond while I was still wondering what the wink was for.

"Double rum thanks to you," replied Alec. We waited. Alec kept on looking at me and grinning and cackling until I was beginning to get rattled. Only the landlord's reassuring looks kept me from leaving the bar. Alec swilled the rum around his glass and swallowed it in two gulps.

"More?" asked Giles. He had another double and began to expand.

"Saw the *'orace* and the *Hecooba*, did yer?" And again I was reminded of the venomous old boatman by the lock.

"Well, you're privileged. Taint everyone that sees old Charlie on his fly run. Lucky you didn't get in 'is way or 'e might of done fer you."

"But there aren't any fly runs these days," I said. The landlord shook his head and I waited for more.

"On the beer, old Charlie was. Did the trip from Guiness to Tyseley in three days flat; just kept going till he got there. Well-nigh killed 'is missus and their young son with the work. Used to go on ahead he did to grab the locks. No one ever got in Charlie's way – too free with 'is iron 'e was. They reckon 'e cracked the skull of old Eli's uncle, Sam Watts, when 'e tried to draw the lock agin him."

"You reckon then that he's still on the beer run?" asked Giles.

"I reckon," Alec replied. "Jest being dead didn't stop he from being on the run. It's in 'is blood so to speak and 'e jest 'as to keep going. But there ain't many as sees him, not nowadays. You were lucky."

Lucky . . . I shuddered. "Have *you* seen him?" I asked.

He turned again to look at me with those black little screwed-up eyes.

"It 'ud be summat if I didn't," he said with another of his cackles. I noted that his wizened lips drew back over a toothless void. "Old 'fly Charlie' were me grandad."

A shiver passed through Steph at the memory of the old boatman. They sat on in silence for a while, still caught up in the web which the story had woven for them.

"Drinks," said Liz. "Happy birthday, Noelle. Happy Christmas all of us," she said, filling glasses and smiling brightly at the other two. Happy . . . happy; she couldn't be more so, she thought, with the two she almost loved most in her tightly organized life. It had to be 'almost', so much of her had died with Patrick and their dead daughter.

"Quite a story," said Noelle. "I think you should publish it."

"Probably," replied her mother. "I don't have the time. Not enough time to do what has to be done."

"*I* couldn't do it." Steph always disclaimed any kind of aptitude for so-called academic work. She'd had her fill at school and university, she said; her clinical reports had always been in arrears. "Lazy," she excused herself. "I'm just bone idle. Prefer my pussies to reading . . . and you know what my letter writing's like."

"Mind if I try it with a few magazines?" asked Noelle. "I've plenty of time in the evenings." She had taken a room with Les and Alice; it saved a tedious journey to work each day and gave Liz more space in the flat.

The story had been published in a women's magazine. Noelle couldn't have been more proud if she had written it herself and the cheque for twenty pounds was propped up on a bookshelf for weeks before Liz noticed it and paid it into Noelle's account.

The Tunnel

Events moved swiftly that following year. Changes and reorganization disrupted the established patterns of colleges and higher education. There were rumours of closures and amalgamations and the first threats to job security began to rustle through the academic corridors; tutors were as edgy as hens when the fox is prowling. Liz was fifty-six, only four years to go before she could retire from the pressures of teaching. She hadn't thought much about it; a cottage in the country she supposed. Rumours became reality on the day when each member of the staff received a carefully worded memo from the LEA. The College would be closed at the end of the academic year; staff employment was guaranteed in other existing colleges.

Liz was offered the option of retirement or transfer to another college in the area. She chose retirement; she felt too old to face the challenge of a different regime, different colleagues, different ideas and practices. She felt deflated; how suddenly the end had come. Where would they live, she wondered.

"Where do you think, Noelle?" she asked the following weekend when Noelle had arrived suddenly and unexpectedly on the Saturday evening. Liz had been too preoccupied with her own affairs to comment.

"No idea at all. What about the canals?" she had replied in a casual off-hand manner, not really caring.

"Listen Liz. I've had a row with Alice and walked out. Was getting fed up anyway. Mind if I go to stay with Steph for a few days – to sort myself out and decide what I'm going to do?"

Liz was jerked back from her own thoughts to an awareness of Noelle's hostility to her mother's lack of interest. There were times when Noelle felt that her mother's concern and care for her were purely academic and that she, Noelle, had been brought up according to the persuasions of the latest child-rearing theories. Steph's natural warmth and genuine concern for the difficulties of others, most especially for those of her friends, very especially for those of Noelle, had often supported and comforted the girl through her growing years when Liz had felt incompetent and slightly bewildered by her daughter's seeming indifference and withdrawal.

"She'll talk to you," Liz had once said rather bitterly when Noelle had packed a case and sought refuge with Steph. "Pity it wasn't you who adopted her." Liz had to battle against her own jealousy, her possessiveness over Noelle. Steph knew of course, but that time she had been angry with Liz.

"Too many students – not enough time for Noelle. How do you think she feels with the flat always filled with students who take up all your attention? You didn't even know she had gone, did you, until twenty-four hours later?"

It was true; it was true now but Liz had learned – with difficulty – to be grateful to Steph for filling in the gaps where she had been inadequate.

"Yes, of course. Go tomorrow. I'll take you to the station. We'll both have to do some thinking about the next moves. Better apart for a few days."

"Thanks, Liz." Noelle was thankful that Liz had agreed so easily, that there had been no tightening of her well shaped mouth, no hint of the old antagonism which used to materialize like a solid wall between them when Noelle would prefer to stay with Steph rather than with Liz.

With Noelle gone Liz considered alternatives, but the decision was already taken and she only reviewed other possibilities as an inconsequential but necessary exercise. If only Steph were on the phone . . . She wrote instead, remembering to enquire first about Noelle and had she come to a decision? Was she all right? How were the cats? How was Steph managing on her small income with the soaring prices? Liz recalled that recently Steph had started something she called a cat hotel. It would pay for the cat food, she had said. At the end of the letter she wrote, "My decision is made. I shall retire gracefully. I hope to invest in a converted narrow boat and shall live on the canals until I get too stiff to jump! I *might* eventually take Noelle's advice and try my hand at writing."

With characteristic precision she immediately began to telephone around the various boat-builders for prices and details of conversions. By the following weekend when she went down to the cottage she had a large folder stacked full with information. She sold the noddy boat, took a holiday in Corfu, made more visits to friends and relations, and it was six months before she saw Noelle and Steph again.

The boat was ready and tied up at Audlem waiting for her return and for its maiden trip. "*Cetus* we'll call it," she said, "after our old butty." All three had planned to take the boat to Weedon to semi-permanent moorings. The cat hotel was thriving and there was a girl from the village who now came in to help; she would stay in the cottage for a week. What about Jan? Liz had written, but Jan couldn't get away, had promised to visit in the spring.

The trip was all they had hoped. The engine, a new Lister HR2 was a dream; push-button start and immediate response.

"That old *Hercules*," said Steph as they remembered.

"She swims well," commented Liz. "So easy to steer."

All too soon the trip was over. On the last evening Noelle told

Liz that she had decided to study for a diploma to qualify for work as a Welfare worker. She and Steph had talked it over. What did Liz think?

"Makes no odds. You're old enough to make up your own mind."

"I could do it at Milton Keynes – catch you on the Cut for holidays – easy to find you – you'll not escape," laughed Noelle, cheerful, optimistic, enjoying this interlude.

Finally Liz was alone except for Simmy the cat, the one she had noticed sitting alone in the cottage, the one that Noelle had found abandoned by the Audlem locks; black and white with a white sneer on the side of its mouth. "Just to remind you of Catty Barnes," Steph said. But this one had been neutered, was docile, had learned to trust its human protectors.

The summer months passed quickly with visits from Noelle and Steph; even Jan managed to escape from her responsibilities. They travelled extensively through the network, tied up at old remembered places. Liz enjoyed her new-found freedom, her expertise on the boat, meeting up with the enthusiasts, talking, living, thinking boats. Had she ever been a respectable and respected teacher, lecturer?

No writing; there didn't seem to be the time. Like the old days of the working boats she thought; I'm just enjoying myself too much.

Autumn days grew shorter and Liz returned to base to make the necessary preparations for winter. She intended still to move along the stretch between Stoke and Buckby, if only to use the engine and to keep the batteries charged. She had grown used to the changes of scenery from the boat's windows and there would be coal to collect from a wharf alongside the Cut near Heyford.

I must get down to writing, she thought. Now or never. I'll tie up on that stretch before Buckby – the Spinneys – nice and quiet and really cut off from casual visitors; there are not even fishermen at this time of the year. She stocked up with tins and packets – plenty of tins for Simmy – collected four bags of coal from Heyford and set off for her retreat.

The Spinneys . . . the Spinneys . . . never tie up under the Spinneys. As she steered the boat along the familiar stretches the old words revived memories of getting the boats stemmed up one dark winter's evening so many years ago.

She had been on the motor; decided to keep going despite the protests of the other two . . . who were they? Marjorie and Susan. She had done one trip with them while waiting for *Hercules* and *Cetus* to be overhauled. Susan, the captain, had wanted to tie up at the Globe but Liz wanted to reach the locks, to be up first in the morning, and had offered to take the motor while the other two steered the butty and made their supper. She had forgotten about the false bend with mud piled on both sides so that it was necessary to steer a middle road instead of taking the outside sweep of the bend. She had stemmed up both boats well and truly under the overhanging trees. Tempers were quickly frayed when working to the point of exhaustion, and Liz knew that her lack of judgement at the end of a hard day was unforgivable – especially as the others had not wanted to continue. They had refused to stay marooned there under the Spinneys and had been forced to shaft and heave their guts out to get the great heavy boats moving again; and when they had reached the locks boats were tied there already. However, they were thankful for a helping hand to catch their ropes and to make fast behind the friendly light of the pair ahead.

"No good travelling at night," Eli had said from the towpath, "specially on that stretch."

Liz had tried to explain.

"Blind Polly said we'd have the locks if we went on. I suppose she thought you'd be gone up through."

"Don't go at night. Can't see the kids." The Nixon brood was legion.

Later in the pub, over beer and rum, the boat people listened to their tale of woe sympathetically.

"You were right not to spend the night under they trees," said one. "None of us ever ties up by the Spinneys. It's a bad place after dark."

"What do you mean exactly?" Susan had asked. "What happens there?"

"Don't rightly know – but we keep going round they bends. None of us ever stops there," he had repeated.

That was all they could find out. In daylight the Spinneys is a delightful stretch with a broad towpath and fields on one side and a tangle of trees and bushes on the other, giving welcome shade from the heat of a summer day.

Later, when occasionally she would meet up with Susan and

Marjorie, they would laugh at the memory of their panic although it was tacitly agreed by them all that the Spinneys was a place to be enjoyed in daylight and to be avoided after dark – for whatever reason. They were boaters, if only 'trainee' boaters, and the beliefs and customs and superstitions of the waterways were inherited along with the way of life they had adopted.

Liz smiled to herself at the images conjured up by her memories. She was passing the ruins of the old cottages where blind Polly used to sit with her knitting. Her brothers had worked on the Cut and, behind the blindness of her eyes, she saw the passing boats; knew almost to the day where each pair was to be located. Pity the cottages had gone along with the old bridge; the new wide one had no character; efficient no doubt and necessary to carry the great weight of traffic in later years.

"Never tie up under the Spinneys". The words re-echoed through her thoughts and memories like a refrain, remembered and then difficult to reject. The warning implicit in the words was tantamount to a challenge. Liz was no longer young and impressionable; she knew the stretch so well that there was no chance of getting her single, powered boat stemmed up as she had done with the heavily laden pair almost thirty years before.

The boat thumped its way through a couple more bridge 'oles, round the false bend and down to the short length of stone coping between the trees which she had come to regard as her own private mooring. It was a tricky manoeuvre to get the boat alongside in that short length but, with a long line from the bows which she snaked along the cabin roof to be within reach, she stepped off from the stern and, with a short shaft ready for emergencies, managed easily. Although she had often tied there on hot summer days she had never spent the night there; no doubt the old superstition was still deeply embedded somewhere in her mind. "Never tie up under the Spinneys"; well, now she'd disprove the threat inherent in the old saw.

She banged in the stakes and the cat sniffed around, exploring the nearby hedge and treading delicately in the damp and rotted undergrowth. Liz stood there watching him, sniffing too the cold, damp air of the winter's day. There would be few, if any, boats travelling at this time of the year and the days of peace and solitude stretched luxuriously before her. Time enough to prove whether or not she had the ability to write up the stories which had begun to sift through her mind in disjointed fragments.

A low flying plane gratingly shattered her thoughts of peace and solitude; with a shrug she started on the chores. Peace and quiet these days were momentary, relative; the phrase a meaningless cliché'd aphorism often used to denote the substitution of one kind of commotion for another. She lifted down a bag of coal from the cabin top. The plane returned in a screaming dive almost overhead so that she instinctively ducked, dropping the bag of coal and spilling some of the contents irretrievably into the water. "Damn . . . damn . . . damn," she said loudly and fiercely. Peace and quiet indeed.

She picked up the remaining coal and humped the bag over the boat side into the well-deck and then buttoned down the cratch cover against the cold and the coming night. Simmy had already returned to the warmer comfort of the cabin. Tea, she thought, teatime, the nicest part of the day. They both settled by the fire, the cat to snooze the hours away and Liz to start on the writing.

The ideas began to sort themselves as she fiddled with the biro, sucked at an orange, poked up the fire, filled a hot water-bottle; anything to delay the moment of commitment when the sheets of paper would have to be filled.

There was the story of the tunnel. Liz finally decided to start on that. It was a horrible story but could well have been possible. The tunnel was still a formidable place, narrow, with the roof irregular and sloping down in places almost onto the cabin roof, but safe enough in these days of regular surveys and careful maintenance. She started to write; it went surprisingly well and the story itself carried her along. It took her three days to complete. For exercise she walked through the wet undergrowth of the Spinneys, over the small bridge and along the towpath between the clumps of dripping ferns and grasses. Simmy came with her, enjoyed the daily walk despite the wet and walked circumspectly in her footsteps. She was glad of his company.

The Cut was deserted at this time of year, and although farms and villages were never far off, the lane of water which threaded through the trees one side and the high hedges on the other seemed separate and remote from the country lanes which led to them over the bridges spanning the water. As she walked, Liz shivered a little at the loneliness of the place, a hidden tunnel under skeletal branches against the greyness of a winter sky. She picked up Simmy and hugged him closely for the solidity and warmth of his familiar shape; but Simmy resisted any prolonged curtailment of his independence and struggled against her efforts to hold him. In the cabin he'd sit for hours on her lap; outside he was Kipling's cat "that walked by his lone self". Liz always felt slightly flattered by his amiability whenever he decided to accompany her.

She decided to spend one more night under the Spinneys to savour more fully the pleasures of solitude. And I'll read through 'The Tunnel', she thought, picking up the stapled pages, although it's probably not as good as I had hoped.

The old tunnel never survived its evil reputation. Built well over a century ago it is now decayed and derelict, a black eyeless socket in the rock face. Through its length a narrow thread of turbid water, almost one and three-quarters of a mile long, burrowed its dark way deep through the unsuspecting countryside. It took the leggers three hours to work each boat through the narrow suffocating tunnel. At places the roof came so low down upon the cabin roof, where the legger crawled like an upside-down mole to propel the boat along, that he was in some danger of being scraped between the two surfaces. He was also in some danger of choking to death in the foul, dank closeness of the middle sections where the air hung thin and sickly above the thread of water. There were other places in the tunnel where, unexpectedly the narrow and confined stretches opened out sideways into thick blacknesses of caves and cuttings where some generation of troglodytes had burrowed and mined for coal and rock in the recesses of the hill. The dark voids in the tunnel wall gave back no echoes from the leggers' slow crawl, gave no hint of any furtive existence which might still survive in the soft pockets of gloom, womb-like and safe from the invasion of light and disclosure. The unknown emptiness opened out for the legger like a featureless field for a blind man so that he was glad to return to the security of the rough, brick-lined surfaces which enclosed him. For one shilling and sixpence a day (7½p) a legger might make three or four such journeys through the underworld. Few boatmen would take their boats through without the 'professional' services of a couple of leggers to lie on their planks and to propel the boat through the long, black length of the tunnel. Some boatmen would have helped the leggers but mostly they sat in their cabins and dozed. It wasn't even possible to brew up the staple diet of tea as the fire had to be doused before entering; the smoke from a fire would have asphyxiated even the hardiest of leggers; and they were by no means a hardy race. The weak, the shiftless, the braggarts, the petty thieves, the violent brawlers, the drunkards and, in fact, the scum of the waterways provided the legging crews for the old tunnel. Unemployable elsewhere, they drifted to the tunnel entrances to be hired by the trip or by the day if they were lucky. Usually the leggers came and went; almost any kind of work was preferable to being immured through the hours of daylight in the narrow length of tunnel, pushing with aching arms and, where the height allowed, with leaden legs like drugged rats unable to escape from the confines of their treadmills.

There's the story of one legger who stuck it out for over a year. He spent all his pay on bad whisky to fuddle himself sufficiently in order to make the next trip through the accursed tunnel. The boat would scrape its way along the side, propelled towards a low half-circle of half-light, finally to emerge into the full gloom of a winter's day or into the hard, fierce light of summer and then to continue a more humane journey through hedgerows and back gardens and dingy streets. A glimpse of such idyllic scenes, a quick drink, a great spitting and belching and the legger must once again adjust his back to the narrow planks of the waiting boat to make a return journey through the worm-hole in the hill while the horse was taken along the pathway over the top. For once the beast had the advantage!

The legger who had lasted for the whole year on a diet of whisky and little else disappeared as unobtrusively as he had arrived. No one knew where and no one particularly cared; he was a joke among his fellows and a byword in the taverns where he was treated to the occasional drink by a boatman who hoped thereby to secure his services in preference to other boatmen waiting for the legger to take them through.

It was small wonder that the tunnel had earned an evil reputation, and small wonder that any man who could find other employment would take it in preference to grovelling through the hours of black entombment. Another story is told of a mean, hard-faced boatman who refused to employ a legger but would force his wretched, fear-ridden wife to work the boat through while he walked the horse over the top. When one day the boat finally emerged from the tunnel where he was waiting, cursing and swearing at her slowness, he found her dead. She was on her back on the cabin top with her legs stuck straight upwards in the air, ossified in her final effort to keep the boat moving; they had to break her legs to put her into the coffin. The treadmill of her existence was perpetuated in her insignificant death upon the cabin roof of her only home, while her mate could only swear at the sorry bargain he'd made in marrying her. She had borne him a child for every one of the eight years that she had endured his attentions and not one child had survived the ensuing birth. After her death it was said that no legger would ever go on his boat so that he was forced to work it through by himself and then to return for the horse. Whether their refusal to leg his boat was a reprisal for past meanness, or whether he was made a scapegoat for their own feelings of guilt in their treatment of the women they bedded with, it is hard to say. Probably their refusal to work for him was rooted in combined feelings of guilt and revenge shot through with superstitious notions that no good would come from her death in such a way. They said that she was not even wearing drawers when the leggers at the far end saw her, only a tattered pair of old boots on her thin, spindly legs and her long black skirt which had fallen back on her stringy groins.

The tunnel was never a success – even as an engineering project – except as one of the first attempts to build a canal tunnel from which to cull experience and knowledge for later and more successful projects. There were frequent falls which imperilled boats and their crews so that, eventually, the tunnel was abandoned completely and a new one built parallel to it. The new tunnel was only a slightly improved version of the earlier attempt. It was slightly longer but it was just as narrow, allowing for the passage of one-way traffic only and the roof, in parts, still sloped down almost to the level of a cabin roof so that the steerer of a boat had to crouch low into the hatchway of the cabin. The towpath crawled alongside the channel; pit-ponies and mules were used to make the dreary journey before bolinders and nationals (engines) replaced the picturesque with the practical. With a towpath allowing the passageway of ponies and mules through the tunnel the leggers gradually became an extinct race.

The Tunnel

This story is about one of them who managed to find employment as mate on a boat carrying sand from Bibby's Wharf at
Lawton to Middlewich. The owner of the boat was a dour,
uncommunicative and wizened little man. The rumour was that
he had done time but had survived the duress of Dartmoor and
had collected his loot which had provided the capital needed for
buying a boat. His talk had a west country slur and was strange to
the ears of the Brummagem and Stoke men who mostly worked
the boats in that area.

Mossey, the legger, was Irish. He'd wandered across the Irish
Sea in one of the annual drifts of immigrants to Liverpool tempted
by the tales of girls and free living away from the restrictions of
church and village censorship. He had worked on the docks and
from there to successive jobs on wharves and waterfronts and
wherever the work and the gin beckoned him. He put the
occasional sentimental thoughts of family and responsibilities
hastily back into the repository of other discomfiting memories;
the tears that misted his rather filmed blue eyes when he sang
'Rose of Tralee' in the gin bars were real enough at the time. So he
lived with his uneasy Catholic conscience by thinking how much
he loved them. Especially he loved them when he hit the top
notes and saw the tears in other Irish eyes; especially he loved
them when he convinced himself and all the other shiftless
drifters that they were doing this for their loved ones, that the
fortunes they would make would buy the farms, pay off the debts
and send the youngest to university. Blissful visions of the
welcome home, of the lives of ease and well-being that awaited
them, made the present more tolerable and their shiftless ways
more acceptable to themselves. They suffered so; how much their
wives and children would never know! Mossey had left his seven
children when the eighth was on its way; left the wretched shack
in the back streets of Dublin when he lost his job at the docks after
a week of celebrating. What he had been celebrating he could
never quite remember; but it had been a very good celebration.

"Want a job?" a harassed looking seaman had shouted from a
small steam ferry as Mossey lounged along the dock frontage
with the other out-of-works. He was tall and tough-looking and
his extra height had caught the skipper's eye. "Shovelling coal on
the old bitch for Liverpool."

Mossey shovelled coal into its belching belly and, once in

71

Liverpool, soon lost himself in the maze of bars and whore-houses. From then on it had been easy to delude himself with good intentions and to keep the loneliness at bay with prossies and nostalgic memories shared with all the others who had exchanged one treadmill for another that was slightly more gaudily painted. For a few years he had been lucky; his strong physique guaranteed him work, first of all on the docks and, later on as he drifted eastwards, on one of the chaingangs employed for building and maintenance work on the canals. He even became a foreman for a few weeks but, after the first bewitchments of power and extra pay had dimmed, the restraints and constraints of his position grew irksome. He was really 'one of the boys'.

"Not the man we thought you to be," the boss had said, and he lost not only his promotion but employment as well. There were a hundred others waiting for his job. From then on he had drifted downwards, tramping and begging between the jobs. He even became a legger for a very brief period. He pushed the boats through in record time and was always in demand. No one realized that it was his panic in the middle sections which lent strength to his efforts. At the start of the worm-hole he'd sing but gradually, as the dark walls closed in around him, the snatches of song would abate into a gasping, panting effort to get the boat and himself out of the accursed hole. In the middle sections where there was not room enough to leg the boat he would splash his way along the uncertain towpath. The stones were slimy and uneven and he had a great fear of slipping down into the murky depths, of being crushed between the boat and the side, of slipping deep into the ooze and the slime. His imaginative fears created shapes and sounds from the dark recesses in the tunnel walls so that he was thankful to leg from the comparative safety of the cabin roof where at all possible. The fear of those middle sections never left him and he began to drink hard at each end in order to face the next trip. The stories of Jack who drank to leg and then legged to drink were still laughed over in the bars, and Mossey had enough sense to recognize Jack's problem as his own. He pulled out before the terrors of drink and darkness overtook him. The handle of a pickaxe was substantial and solid, and the sun on his back felt good after the troglodyte existence of the previous few weeks. His eyes had become filmed and rheumy and his fine dark beard was now ragged and dirty; but he was still able to wield a pickaxe with a semblance of his old strength and also to lead the choruses after a couple of gins.

Loading bricks was an easy respite after hacking at the limestone faces through the hot summer days and Mossey felt almost happy in the easy repetitive pace of piling his hod, balancing across the gangplank to the boats and stacking the bricks in their beds of straw. He was one of the casuals who had been sent over from the quarries to help with the loading. He was stripped off to his ragged trousers and his weather-browned torso was still impressive despite the flab. The skinny man with the pinched face and sharp, restless eyes watched him carefully as he loaded.

"Want a change of job?" he asked later as the men sat in the shade of a hut by the water. They all knew him as Skinny, an obvious derivative from Mr Skinner; it was also a pretty fair description of the narrow, sharp little man whose eyes were everywhere but who never looked at anyone directly. Sometimes he was known as Shifty, but it was always Mr Skinner to his face from gaffers and workmen alike. He was a 'number one' and that earned respect in days when few men enjoyed the privilege of working for themselves. The real bosses lived in the big houses away from the sordid business of dealing with the men; they employed the tough, hard-faced men to do that for them. So Mr Skinner, as a number one who owned but also worked his own boat, enjoyed an unusual degree of respect on the Cut. Presumably his ill-gotten gains had paid off – eventually. He had established a fairly regular contract for carrying sand and bricks from Lawton to Stoke. The two-way trip took a day and it irked him that he had to bring the boat back empty. Skinny was looked upon with suspicion by the bosses and, no doubt, his reputation as an ex-convict was known to most of them so that he'd had to work hard and to accept the one-way trips in order to get established. It was never really known that he'd been in Dartmoor, but it was a convenient tale that explained Skinny's comparative wealth and his secretive, almost furtive, mannerisms and habits. Sometimes he slept on the boat but it was rumoured that he had a cottage somewhere in the Middlewich area where he kept a young wife well hidden from the lechery of the casual labouring gangs. It was even rumoured that he kept her chained up in the cottage while he was away. Whatever the truth of the matter no one ever knew for certain that he had a cottage, or where it was, or who lived in it. Skinny would walk away over the hill of the tunnel and return the same way. No one ever attempted to follow him; there was a wariness and an alertness about the man which kept the most aggressive and the most inquisitive at a distance. It was known that he carried a seaman's knife in a special leather slip pocket of his jacket; he used it often enough in the daily work of his boat but it was an evil looking blade; more of a weapon than a tool. It was said that he had used it in a scuffle over some money he was thought to have owed one of the men, and the man had never recovered from the wounds. A reputation was soon established from certain early impressions and then embellished in the competitive tale-telling smoke of the alehouse. Skinny did and said nothing to contradict the tales that he knew were told of him. His reputation earned for him what he most desired, an immunity from any real contact with any of them.

Although the bosses still disliked and mistrusted him as a person, they soon recognized the fact that he was efficient and reliable and his boat was seldom idle for long. He had now been offered a really good contract; bricks to Middlewich and salt back from Middlewich to Stoke; three trips a week and the rates were very good. Skinny had his own reasons for accepting the contract apart from the money and the prospect of a regular run; he'd be better able to keep an eye on his cottage in Middlewich. He was an ambitious little man and, like Mossey, he too had dreams of returning to his homeland with success and fortune to flaunt in the faces of those who had despised him and had politely ignored his existence as one of the lower classes who wasn't even suitably grateful for the charity given to his mother and five brothers after his father had died from a virulent attack of influenza. He ran off to sea when he was only twelve to escape from the heaviness of a law weighted against the young offender in the hope of deterring him for the rest of his life from the sin of envy, the envy of those who lived in the house where his mother scrubbed while the 'family' wined and dined oblivious of her aching back. He had stolen a brooch which one of the young ladies had unpinned in the kitchen and which she had left forgetfully lying on a shelf of the dresser. He had been bringing in the carrots from the garden and it had been all too easy to pocket the bauble. Directly he had taken it into the town's pawnbroker on market day he knew that he'd mistaken the strength of the network geared against the poor and desperate. He hadn't waited for the knock on the door or to see the bitter set of his mother's mouth; he had left them without word or letter. He could barely write his name. For thirty years he had worked and saved, determined not to be crushed by the injustices of poverty. The life at sea hardened and sharpened him; he became ship's carpenter and learned the rudiments of a trade which he later turned to good account when he left the sea to work for a cabinet-maker in Bristol. The old man, his new employer, had also been a ship's carpenter in his youth and the two of them lived and worked together in the small, back-street premises. Skinny and his employer were never friends, never exchanged confidences; neither knew anything of the other except in the daily business of working and eating. At sea both had learned the necessity for inwardness, the canny suspicion of all others which was a defence for survival, and the sharp awareness of all incident and detail which ensured the survival to be profitable.

The old man died. Skinny sold the business and also inherited the nest-egg of just over two hundred pounds which he had always known was stuffed into the old man's mattress. There had been more than enough to buy his boat and to help him through the months of suspicion which had met him like a wall. He knew that money was to be made in canal porterage and so he persevered with the small inconvenient contracts until the more regular work came his way. He was glad, too, to be working once again in the open air; the years of being confined in the back-street workshop had been necessary but he had missed the sharpness of wind and spray on his face and the openness of space around him. He was too old to return to the sea, but a boat of his own on the canals which were fast developing in the Midlands was a good compromise. It had been a dream which had often sustained him during the long silent hours of working with plane and saw. He knew that he would not leave the old man while he lived, not only for the money he would inherit when the old man died, but for some unspoken, unacknowledged feeling of comradeship and dependency which existed between them.

The old man's death had been quiet and sudden; alive one day and dead the next morning when Skinny had been surprised not to see him already at work. There had been a sense of loss, soon followed by relief; he was free to buy his boat, to be his own boss, to make the fortune he felt was now within his reach. He bought shrewdly: the boat; a good horse already trained for work with a boat; and a small cottage in Middlewich with a shed in which to stable the horse. Money in a mattress was too risky a proposition and it was better invested in property; he knew that he could have made off with the old man's savings years ago. Skinny had learned, however, that long-term plans can often be more profitable than more immediate gains; he had known that the old man's hoard was safe and it had suited him to wait. Occasionally he thought of his mother and younger brothers, but dispassionately as a part of his youth that was sour and unpalatable in his memory. He'd go back when he was ready and, if his mother was still alive, he'd make provision for her.

Meanwhile he had this contract; bricks to Middlewich and salt back to Stoke. In ten years, if the contract held, his calculating brain predicted that he'd have enough, enough to buy out the family his mother had skivvied for and enough to keep him and her in real luxury. This run also meant that he'd be able to spend every other night in his Middlewich house and so keep an eye on everything. At Stoke he'd sleep in The Boat, a canalside pub where the housewife kept a clean bed and made no demands upon his reticence. She was a widow on the defensive for her reputation and, although The Boat was on the Cut, she kept an orderly house. Skinny had stayed there occasionally and felt a twinge of kinship with the tight-lipped, scrawny woman in her severe black dress, relieved only by a heavy necklace of black jet, worn as if to reinforce the impression of perpetual mourning. Had he been the marrying kind he once thought . . . but he wasn't. His purpose was set and not even the respectable order of Mrs Aston's table and household could tempt him. However, he had it in his mind to offer the use of his boat cabin to the mate he would need to employ; it would save him paying the man full wages. He would need someone reliable to get the boat through the tunnel each trip. The horse knew its way over the top and, in any case, there were always urchins ready to earn a precious farthing for walking with the horse and holding it at the further end until the boat should emerge. The new tunnel had a wash of water which was pumped through at intervals to help the progress of the boats, but there was still some heavy hauling to be done to propel the boat through without too much loss of time. There were also thirty or more locks between the tunnel and Middlewich and, if he was to keep on schedule, he'd need the help of a strong man. Skinny himself was no longer young and, although he could do a day's steering with the best, the effort required for continuous locking was beginning to tell and Skinny had no intention of putting his health at risk before he had achieved the goal he had set for himself. To hire a man might add a few extra years to the completion of his plans, but it seemed to the careful Skinny a better guarantee of success. He remembered the years of waiting in Bristol; he was good at waiting. A man on board would also act as a guard in Middlewich where a boat could soon lose its cargo if left unattended for any length of time. Skinny had weighed up the advantages and disadvantages of hiring a mate and his mind was made up; his only problem was to find the right man. He had noticed Mossey first of all because of his build; he could be strong if he cut down on the drink and ate two good meals a day. He had the look of a man defeated by the odds stacked against him. Skinny knew the look only too well; the faces of most labourers carried its stamp. Some were grey and apathetic, some were coarse with a show of filth and brutality, and some were sly with a simple cunning; but the look was the same. Skinny watched the Irishman closely. Another year and the apathy and despair would finish him. His self-respect would be lost in the gin bottle and after that his physique would deteriorate rapidly. Skinny could foresee his fate and despised him. As he worked Mossey would still burst out with a snatch of song while the others swore and spat and belched or farted. His Irish voice still carried an echo of the old magic with which he had once charmed his family and pub audiences. Perhaps it was the voice which finally decided Skinny to offer him the job. A song was preferable to the loud-voiced cursing which was the common language of most navvies.

"Two shillings a week, a cabin, your food and two pairs of boots a year," he said.

Mossey was amazed. Why should Skinny – Mr Skinner – choose to employ him? A small grip of hope held him speechless. Then his eyes narrowed with a learned a suspicion of such offers.

"What's the snag? Too good to be true to a bloke you don't know."

"On the level. No drink. That's the snag. I want the work done and done regular. No days off. No gin. Up to you."

Two or three of the men had stopped to listen and it was obvious to Mossey that if he refused there were many who would think he was crazed and would promise anything for such an offer. Boots as well.

"Same as farm labourers," added Skinny. "But no drink."

"Thanks, Mr Skinner. I promise about the booze."

He wasn't too certain of his promise and Mr Skinner knew that his voice held little conviction; but a hard day's work – probably fourteen hours a day – and good food would probably swing the odds. Skinny was a passable cook and believed in the value of simple but nourishing food. He himself ate sparingly but sensibly.

"Tea after you've finished loading," said Mr Skinner, "and we'll talk about the job."

The 'talk' lasted fifteen minutes. Skinny had drawn a simple but explanatory map of the route, the locks, the tunnel, the loading and offloading wharves.

"The tunnel," Mossey groaned. "Every day the tunnel. Three hours of the bloody dark."

"Partly why I need a mate. You've legged the tunnel; should be used to it. You pull and I steer."

"Not on the bloody towpath. You get yourself a mule. Not me."

"If I get a mule you'd have to lead it."

Finally they arranged to take turns in the tunnel and to propel the boat in whatever way best suited each of them. The horse would go over the top as usual. Skinny insisted that both of them were needed on the boat; the tunnel and the locks were his main reasons for hiring Mossey as a mate.

Mossey was still uncertain. The thought of the tunnel made him want to retch but Skinny's cold wariness was reassuring. The job would be regular; the conditions were the best he could hope for and his only 'boss' would be Skinny who was no kind of a boss at all, just a worker like himself. Skinny was a number one though; in time perhaps he too would own a boat and they'd work a pair. Already the future assumed pleasant possibilities in his wishful and fertile imagination.

"Start next Monday. Give your notice to the gaffer today;

you're paid by the day so there's no problem. I pay you on Saturdays, night-time so you can't spend it. Sundays you need to lie in, clean out the cabin, scrub the hold if the cargo's been shifted, check the ropes, oil the sidecloths, make sure that the boat is ready for the week. I look after the horse." It was typical of Skinny's relationships with people and animals alike that he never gave a name to his horse as did most of the boat people; it was always 'the horse' or 'it'.

So it was arranged. Mossey had a final blow-out of his wages in the pub on Saturday night.

"Last time," he said with maudlin self-pity. "Old skinflint will work the hide off me. No booze, no women, juss work."

They supported him in his self-pity, but any one of them would have cut him out given the chance. Skinny was close and tough but fair; he'd work hour by hour with Mossey and that was something they'd all respect. Mossey sensed their envy and, because he was generous in his newly-found promise of security, he spent his last shillings on drinks for them all.

"Me last farewell," he shouted and broke into 'Mother Mac-ree'. He'd forgotten most of the words but that was no problem to Mossey, he just fitted whatever words came into his gin-stimulated brain. The evening was a grand success – a topic of conversation for long afterwards.

"Remember that evening in the old Black Cow?" they'd ask him; but, by then, he had no memory for such carefree pleasures. The gin which they bought for him evoked horrors beyond telling although, if he drank enough, the horrors would gradually dissolve into a soporific drowsiness so that his night's sleep would be heavy and untroubled. When he awoke the blessed daylight would have come again. His mates who had known him in happier times bought him the gin that was fast destroying him; it was all they could do.

The partnership worked well. Mossey lost much of his flab, grew cheerful and optimistic again despite the fourteen or sixteen hours a day of strenuous work; not so strenuous as he grew more fit and his body more used to the work expected from it. His voice regained some of its past richness and, although his repertoire was limited and repetitive, it pleased them both. Skinny was content with his bargain but was careful not to show it; he kept his distance. During the day the boatwork kept them apart and, at the end of the day after a final look round, he gave Mossey any instructions he thought necessary and was away to his house in Middlewich or to his room in Mrs Aston's inn. Saturday nights were the hardest for Mossey. They were always tied in Middlewich and the Saturday evening sounds of booze and women were hard to resist. There were times when he cursed Skinny with every oath he knew and swore he'd have his fling come what may. Skinny used to sense these times and would return to the *Juniper* on the pretext of checking some detail but, as the weeks passed, it seemed to him that he was having to check on Mossey more often than was prudent. One night he brought down a bottle of gin for Mossey. "To celebrate," he said abruptly in response to Mossey's look of suspicion and surprise, although he gave no further explanation of what the celebration was about. They both had a brief drink together and then Skinny had left after putting the bottle away in the cupboard. "Enough there for a few celebrations," he had said. Mossey had resisted for an hour or so, but then had succumbed. He had emptied the bottle so quickly that he vomited and then fell into a state of semi-stupor. Skinny had returned and stayed the rest of the night with him. His cold threat of dismissal the next morning had a sobering effect. Usually they reached Middlewich late in the evening and the bricks would not be offloaded until early Monday morning. It was imperative for Mossey to remain sober in order to keep guard through the weekend; he threw the empty bottle overboard in disgust and swore he'd never again touch a drop of the stuff. He often spoiled for a fight and sometimes had occasion to use his fists. The pilferers along the Cut were always on the look out for easy loot which they could sell for a few pence and bricks were always a popular target. It was not difficult to lift a few at a time and to hide them under a jacket or in an old sack and then to sell them on the streets or in the back yards. However, Mossey's fists and quick ears soon became known and the *Juniper* was left alone.

Skinny gave Mossey bonus money when he got a good price himself, and he opened a bank account for Mossey, an unheard of arrangement for a labourer at that time.

"I'll pay it in direct," he said. "Better than carrying loose money around on a boat. You won't need much; no time for spending. In a year you'll have a week's holiday and there'll be money enough in the bank to take you to Ireland. In five years you'll have enough to buy a cottage. Property's the thing. Keeps your money safe."

Mossey accepted the arrangements easily enough and even began to adopt Skinny's habits and aims as his own.

The only problem was the tunnel. Mossey dreaded those three hours of immurement each day – more rather than less.

"It's not natural," he'd say. He didn't know of claustrophobia, but that was his trouble. He enjoyed his work along the open stretches; he began to take a pride in the appearance of the boat and to assume responsibility for right loading. It was his kind of life – the tunnel apart. The sight of that small black hole in the hillside turned his stomach and he stayed sick and breathless throughout the whole length of it until they re-emerged into the daylight. Skinny was very good about it although he insisted that Mossey should always stay aboard rather than take the horse over the top. Perhaps he hoped that Mossey's fear of the tunnel would be cured eventually through growing familiarity with its contours and peculiar sounds and echoes.

He trudged most of the way on the partially sunken towpath pulling the heavy boat behind him; no point in hiring a mule with two strong men aboard and his own horse had not been trained for the tunnel work. It was a good horse, strong and even-tempered, reliable and well trained for the lock work but, like Mossey, was terrified of the black gloom of the tunnel. He was too good a horse to change and so Skinny either left him to take the path over the top or paid on urchin to accompany him while he took over the towing line on the stretch through the underground. Mossey would do his best to steer in the half-circle of light from the lantern lashed to the bows and to keep the boat from scraping the sides, but where the tunnel roof came down low over the boat he'd have to rush down into the cabin where a candle gave light and reassurance. Then Skinny would yell at him to come out and to straighten up the stern so that he could continue pulling from the bows. Their shouting would echo and rebound through the hollow blackness like lost souls in the underworld; but it was the shouting which helped Mossey to keep going.

There were better days when he did some of the towing, although he felt dreadfully vulnerable alone on the towpath with the laps of water from the 'waves' washing over his boots. He was terrified of slipping and edged along by the wall, equally terrified of the damp, semi-luminous patches of orange and pink slimy fungus which scabbed the walls at intervals. They were quicker with Skinny's steadier pace although the boat crashed less often with him steering. With bricks it was necessary not to crash the boat; the bricks were brittle and the broken ones rejected and counted against the payment for transport.

They were carrying salt from Middlewich and, on coming to the entrance of the tunnel, Mossey became almost hysterical about going through. The hot sun which he had been cursing an hour back as they worked through the Lawton flight of locks now seemed totally desirable. The black hole ahead was to him like the entrance to hell. They waited at the side as a boat coming from the southern end of the tunnel crawled back into the light. It was a stone boat (carrying stone) worked by Jed, a red-headed bastard who stayed at the tiller while his wife worked the locks and towed the boat through the tunnel. Luckily, one or the other was infertile so that there were no children to sap her strength. Jed left no one in doubt which of the two he considered was to blame for the lack of children and his treatment of her reflected his resentment. She accepted the blame and was thankful he still kept her. She emerged from the tunnel blinking in the light, the towing line a wet streak across her shoulder and round her waist. Her long black skirt was hitched up into its waistband and the unlaced boots slopped water over her skinny legs. She saw the waiting boat and let down her skirt.

"That's right, Lil," laughed Jed. "Don't let 'em see yer privates. Bad enough fer me."

Lil was used to his coarseness and threw the towing line back across the boat ignoring Mossey as he leaned against the bows of the *Juniper* trying to force himself to look into the hole instead of back into the sunlight.

"Tunnel's bad today," said Jed to Skinny. "Lots of water pouring through the side. About halfway through. Not on the towpath side though. Keep yer cabin doors shut or it'll drown yer."

Skinny had himself sheeted up the precious cargo against possible rain; salt was a tricky cargo and Skinny always insisted upon safety measures.

"Bloody tunnel. Bloody 'orrible 'ell-place," muttered Mossey, but Skinny appeared not to be at all bothered by Jed's warning.

"Looks as if you got a wetting," said Mossey looking sideways at Jed as they passed.

"In the cabin an' all," said Jed. "Saw it too late and of course she's too dim to give us the warning."

Lil was waiting by the couple of mules tied on the bank, stroking their soft muzzles and ignoring the man and the boats.

The door of the small pump-house opened and a short man with a shock of cropped white hair appeared.

"Free to go through now, Mr Skinner," he shouted. "I'll get the pump going to give you a ride."

"Better watch that tunnel of yours," Jed yelled at him. "Water pouring through the wall in the middle there. Better get it looked at. Bad as the old tunnel this one is – never safe either on 'em."

"We'll get off then, Mr Jones," said Skinny sharply and ignoring Jed. "You get aboard, Mossey." He knew the effect Jed's words would have upon the already reluctant Mossey.

"I'll pull," said Mossey stubbornly. "For the first bit anyway." He hated to think the bugger Jed might sniff out his fear.

They slid forwards into the hole. The obedient horse took its own way along the narrow pathway and disappeared through the bushes which bristled over the top like thatch on an eyeless face. Slowly, as the first wave lifted them, Mossey took up the slack and they were swallowed into the darkness of the underground. Mossey had lit the lantern and strapped it securely to the rings at the base of the cratch where it was safe from being crashed by any obstruction. He'd put in a new wick and the light was quite good.

"Keep yer eyes on the arc of the beam. Don't look down. Yez all right Mossey, yez all right." He repeated Skinny's advice to himself over and over and then started to sing. He felt fine and his panic had left him. He trudged on, keeping the songs echoing around and about the dripping walls. The waves sent by the pump made the work easy; it was not so much that he was needed for towing the boat but rather that he kept the bows straight while Skinny corrected the drift of the stern with the tiller. The darkness grew thicker but the light was steady. Mossey kept his eyes on the arc which it shed on the curve of the walls. Even when he felt one of the tunnel rats drop from a ledge in the brickwork onto his boot he still kept his eyes upwards. It was a rat, just a rat; he knew there were hundreds of them hidden away in the cracks and crevices of the walls. They'd be scared of the light like he was scared of the dark. His singing changed to whistling and 'Rose of Tralee' filtered shrilly through the gap in his front teeth. The roof began to narrow downwards.

Skinny called out, "Doing well today, Mossey. Come aboard and I'll take over. Nearly halfway. Come and get your tea." They kept a couple of bottles of cold tea ready to wash down the gritty murk of the tunnel as they went.

"Think I can hear that waterfall ahead, what Jed told us of," said Mossey as he stepped onto the counter, pleased with himself that he had kept his panic at bay for so long.

"Keep the cabin doors shut then," said Skinny taking his place on the towpath. "It's on your side. Don't want to get the cabin flooded. Have your tea when we're the other side of it. Better check on the top sheets as well."

Mossey edged round the gunwale to make certain that the corner of the top sheet was securely fastened. The salt was in sacks and packed up on boards with more cloths packed over and around the sacks; Skinny took no chances.

"All right," he shouted back.

"Better get going then," said Skinny as he picked up the slack of rope and went ahead.

The waves carried them forwards and the bows scraped and banged along the edge of the narrow towpath until Skinny was able to push them straight again. The tunnel was something less than ten feet wide; the towpath was two feet, which left almost nothing for manoeuvring the seven-foot width of the boat. The men who worked the company boats never bothered themselves about the scrapings and the bangings. They sat in the cabins and played cards, and drank when they could afford to do so, as the pumped waves edged them through. Occasionally a boat would become jammed against the side; the men were quick to shove it off again before the boat could spring a leak. A boat could sink quickly, especially if loaded with an absorbent cargo such as salt. There were many tales of boats being sunk after crashing in the narrow width of a bridge'ole, with loss of boat, loss of cargo and even loss of life. None of the boatmen could swim and, in places, the water was deep enough to drown a grown man, especially if he panicked. The tunnel was no place for such a disaster.

Mossey heard the splash of water ahead, a real waterfall. He pulled the hatch cover over more securely and checked that the doors were properly closed. "Wonder where it's from?" he thought, vaguely apprehensive. "Must be a leak from the old tunnel and a pile-up in one of the cavities." It all happened as he was speculating. There was a great rush of sound from the crash ahead as the boat stemmed hard onto the pile-up of bricks and rock and from the rush of water which lifted the boat until the tunnel roof came down hard upon the cabin top. Mossey fell flat across the small stern deck and grabbed the tiller neck with both hands.

As suddenly as the boat lifted it dropped as a great wave of water freed from the gaping hole in the tunnel wall rushed back towards the outlet. Mossey slowly staggered to his feet. Some of the falling debris had smashed the glass of the headlamp and the front of the boat was in complete darkness. A faint glimmer of light from the candle still miraculously alight and upright in the cabin flickered through the thick glass of the porthole. Another thump of falling rock thudded on to the side sheets and lurched the front end free from its impacted obstruction.

Skinny. Where was Skinny?

"Mr Skinner," he yelled, "You all right, Mr Skinner?"

"Here," came Skinny's voice from somewhere up in the darkness. "Up here. Help . . . I'm hurt. Hanging onto the topstrings. My leg's hurt. Come and give us a hand."

"Coming. Hang on. Must get a light. Hang on."

Tentatively Mossey opened a door into the cabin. The water had stopped pouring from the gash in the wall and the boat seemed to be safe for the moment. He remembered that there was a hurricane-lantern under one of the sidebeds; if only there were enough oil in it to get it alight.

"Hang on," he called again from the open door of the cabin. "Getting the lantern."

"Hurry . . . Hurry . . . Oh God . . ." came Skinny's voice, rising to something like terror.

Mossey heard them too, the plops of dozens of bodies dropping against the top sheets and onto the roof of the cabin. There must be hundreds of them, he thought wildly. Shut the cabin doors, but already two or three of them had dropped through onto the cabin floor. Christ! Holy Jesus! What were they? Rats he could face; but these . . . they were pink and hairless with two enormous gnawing fangs and hard, unwinking eyes. They were long and lean with their rib cages showing through their almost transparent skin. They rushed between his legs and disappeared behind the coal box. He heard them scrabbling beneath the floor boards.

"God! Christ! Skinny! My God, Skinny!" he gasped. If that was what he could hear falling all around him on the boat outside what was happening to Skinny?

Skinny's voice cut through his panic and the silence, a silence punctuated by plops and further occasional falls of bricks into the water.

"For God's sake Mossey, quick. They're gnawing my hands. I can't move. Quick, you bastard!" His voice ended in a shriek of pain and terror.

Somehow Mossey found the lantern and somehow he got it alight. He'd have to go out there. He couldn't. He was safe enough here in the cabin. Those two or three under the floor boards – he could deal with them; but all those others, hundreds of them. He and Skinny would be eaten alive. How could he even get out there without opening the doors? Holy Mother of Jesus; he crossed himself as he had been taught as a child. The fear in him was too great. Skinny would have to take his chance.

"Mossey, for Christ's sake, a light. Bring a light. They're scared of light."

Skinny, how could he leave Skinny? It could have been him out there and Skinny in the cabin.

"Skinny. I'm coming," he yelled. "Hang on."

"Hurry . . . Hurry." A further yell and a scream of pain and fear cut through the cabin walls.

Mossey clutched harder at the lantern and clamped the teeth in his dry mouth. He pushed the lantern ahead of him and flung open the cabin doors against the resistance of bodies on the stern deck. Out; he was out and the doors slammed shut again. The pink, hairless bodies retreated as he pushed the light towards them. He swung the light out over the towpath. "Christ! not there," he whispered, "not down there." The narrow path was alive with them running blindly backwards and forwards, jostling and crawling over each other in heaps. He shone the lantern over the cabin top; not so many there. They tended to drop off as they landed but they were still jumping out from the gaping wound in the tunnel side. They landed on the top planks and on the sides of the sheeted boat; the few who made it to the cabin top did so by luck.

They're blind, thought Mossey. Can't see where they're going. Don't like the light for some reason . . . "Coming. Hang on. Over the top," he shouted. There was no answer, but Mossey barely noticed in his own fearful concentration to keep clear of the dagger-like fangs. He crawled along the cabin roof pushing the lantern ahead of him. The bodies scrambled away from the light to fall over the sides into the water or onto the seething mass on the towpath. The boat was almost stationary now; no more following waves. Mr Jones at the pump-house or someone else must have realized that something was wrong and Mossey felt slightly cheered at the thought of imminent rescue.

The roof of the tunnel was so low that Mossey could only crawl along the top planks. He tucked his head down into the collar of his jacket in mortal fear that one of the creatures would land in his hair. A couple landed on his back, but he was able to brush them off against the rough bricks of the roof. The nightmare crawl continued until at last he saw Skinny in the flickering, uncertain light from the lantern. There was very little oil left and the fear of being marooned in the darkness at the mercy of those gnawing fangs lent further urgency to his movements. Skinny was clinging desperately to the top strings of the cratch cover, his feet hanging over the side of the boat completely hidden in the mass of crawling bodies.

"God in heaven help him," muttered Mossey, his own fears temporarily forgotten in his horror at Skinny's plight. The bodies were using Skinny's head and back for footholds, clinging to the cloth of his jacket and trousers. In the light from the lantern Mossey saw the gnawing movement of their fangs and heard the grate of teeth against canvas and wood. One of the creatures was gnawing away at Skinny's clenched fist. Mossey had grabbed one of the heavy iron mooring stakes from the cabin roof and he had the small satisfaction of knocking the slimy beast from poor Skinny's hand. He tried to dislodge those from his back but they hung on tenaciously.

"I'll grab yer arms and yank you up here," he shouted. "Must fix the light first."

Skinny looked up for the first time; he'd tried to protect his face. "Hurry," he muttered. Mossey lay down along the top planks to give himself a better hold and swung the lantern over the front end of the cratch to fix the handle through the end of rope which still held the smashed headlamp.

The lantern shed its small gleam of light ahead and into the gash in the wall. He had a swift impression of the channel half blocked by bricks and rock and then, the further horror overtook him. Instinctively he edged backwards as the shape slithered along below the gleam of light. His horror obliterated all sense, all awareness of the rats, of Skinny's plight, even of his own danger; the whole concentration of his terror was upon the thing that was pouring itself out of the gaping hole. He had no thought for Skinny, not even for the rats that squirmed under him as he edged slowly backwards. Coil after coil of it wound from the hole and along the towpath, swallowing the rats as it came. They made no sound except for their scrabbling and their gnawing. The coils were of the same pinkish, whitish colour as the rats. It was something that had grown for a long time in the dark recesses of underground pools and cavities far away from the light; the eternal worm that lives in darkness.

Mossey saw the bulge of the rats through its skin and through the shell-like ribs and muscle frame as it swallowed its way through the writhing mass on the towpath. Every now and then it paused and lifted a flattened head which swayed in the soft beam of the lantern. It couldn't see either; the thought registered through Mossey's mind without him being aware of it. It could reach up and touch him if it would; he had no will left to move further. It had reached Skinny, at least the head was now close to where Skinny still hung, more dead than alive, clutching the last frayed edges of canvas which was being gnawed to shreds by the machine-like motion of the army of teeth. His head hung below his sunken neck. The rats left him as their devourer slid nearer. It reached Skinny, flicked a long tongue over his inert back and moved on. Mossey heard his own gasp of relief and the flicker of a dead hope that he might yet heave Skinny to a kind of safety licked through his almost insensate mind. Then the head turned and writhed back upon itself. It flicked again at Skinny's back, his neck and his gnawed wrists. It slid upwards and nudged Skinny almost gently, so that the rigid grip loosened and Skinny's body fell quickly and easily onto the coils below. Mossey saw the coils wrap themselves softly and carefully around Skinny and then ease back with their burden, back into the wall opening.

Mossey remembered nothing more. He must have crawled instinctively back into the cabin. The rats meant nothing to him after the last vision of horror. He was back in the cabin, the doors closed and padlocked, the candle still burning. He could see nothing but that last glimpse of Skinny's face; there had been no eyes. Mossey prayed that he was dead.

He sat there, head sunk in hands. One of the rats had emerged and began to gnaw at his boot. He lashed out at it with his foot and it squashed easily. He wondered dully why he had been so afraid of them. The candle was burning low and was guttering in pools of grease from the slight draught in the cracks of the doors. There were no more candles, he remembered; when this one died he'd be in darkness and in the darkness the thing would again emerge. The cabin sides looked pitiably fragile and inadequate; would they resist the pressures from such a monster? Mossey gibbered remembered fragments of prayers; Joseph, Mary and Jesus – would they ever hear him? Where was Jones and the rescue team? They should have arrived by now. They would never arrive; Joseph, Mary and Jesus would never hear him from the depths of this hell-hole; the serpent was the devil himself come for Mossey's soul – for his body too if he could believe what had happened to Skinny. He thought of his family, Mary and all of his eight children deserted by him and left to fend for themselves. Why hadn't he sent the money which he had promised? Why hadn't he gone to see them in those early days when there had been money in his pockets? Why hadn't he written or got one of the gaffers to write for him? He remembered with anguish the times when he had denied having a family, when he had laughed with the other fickle and plausible deserters at their canny ruses for evading the marriage trap. He agonized in his remorse while he waited for the inevitable end. If only Mary could see him now, surely she'd forgive him? But perhaps she had found another man, another protector; she had been sharp and bright enough even after the toils of childbearing; but eight hungry mouths to fill . . . Mossey sank deep into his misery, hunched on the side bed with his legs drawn up under him. The candle was almost burnt out with the wick sporadically flickering in its pool of grease on the top of the stove. The gnawing continued endlessly so that Mossey expected the wooden sides of the cabin to disintegrate with their relentless onslaught. He started to shiver and he was aware that his trousers were wet, soaked with urine as well as with the Cut water. A fire; a small spark of hope, struck from the need to survive despite all the odds, penetrated his misery. There was coal in the coal-box and dry sticks. Skinny was always adamant about keeping the cabin clean with everything ready for use. If only he could get the fire going before the candle finally extinguished. There was a bag of dry shavings under the stove. As he pulled it out another of the rats fell from it and scuttled away to a corner of the cabin where it faced Mossey with its yellow unwinking stare. Mossey ignored it; he'd deal with it later; the fire was the thing and the only hope left for him; it would give smoke and light as well as heat. The chimney was down and Mossey prayed that the vent on the cabin top had not been blocked by falling debris. Surprisingly none of the rats had ventured to explore the opening. He emptied most of the shavings into the empty grate and scooped up some of the solidfied candle grease. There were sticks in the coal-box and plenty of coal; enough to last the night and a full day if necessary.

Mossey worked with care; it would be difficult enough to get a good blaze going with the tunnel roof almost hard down on the cabin top so that there would be hardly any escape for the smoke and little enough draught in the tunnel itself. The sticks caught easily and carefully Mossey began to pile on the coal. It was good just to see the blaze from the sticks and to feel the heat on his face and hands. At first the smoke poured back down into the cabin; if only he dared to open the doors. He undid the bolt and opened one side for the merest crack; luckily the doors opened outwards and Mossey was able to hold it firm. It was enough to draught up the blaze and to catch the coal. Thankfully Mossey rebolted the doors and stood hunched and bent – for he was a tall man and the cabins were less than his six feet in height – to dry off his trousers and to draw what comfort he could from the warmth. There was water too in the kettle and Mossey found the thought of tea more pleasurable than all the gin in which previously he had drowned his fears and his sorrows.

He began to think more clearly and to wonder if he might yet

escape from this hell-hole, this dank and evil place with its foul
inhabitants. What was the time of day – or of night? He had no
means of knowing, no way of assessing the number of hours that
the boat had been marooned here. Surely Mr Jones would have
noted their failure to emerge at the further end, although it was
unlikely he'd enquire. The horse would wait patiently for an hour
or so and then go quietly cropping where it could find grass
enough; no one would interfere with it. It was Mr Skinner's horse
and no one interfered with Mr Skinner's affairs. The sounds from
the rats became a steady background to his thoughts. When he
heard the gnawing at the cabin itself he beat the sides and the roof
with the back of the coal shovel and the sounds of teeth scraping
would withdraw for a time. The kettle began to hiss and the cabin
was warm although stuffy and smelling strongly of dried urine
and sweat; not that Mossey noticed. He found the tea and put the
pot on the edge of the stove to warm. He slashed at the rat which
had left its corner to return to the darker refuge behind the
coal-box. He missed, but it could wait. Tea would restore his
courage and his strength.

The gnawing and scraping had grown fainter and Mossey was
resigned to sitting out the waiting time until rescue should come.
If he could keep the fire going and not fall asleep there was a
chance. He shut his mind to thoughts of Skinny; the thoughts
were too horrible to bear and each time that the memory of
Skinny's face and his last cry for help returned to him Mossey
submerged the memory in a welter of repeated fragments of
prayers dredged up from his Catholic childhood. He held the
teapot ready then stiffened, listening. He would have welcomed
the now familiar sounds of the rats. He half-turned to watch in
hideous fascination the slow, barely perceptible undulations
covering the opaque glass of the porthole. Slowly, he felt the
great sinuous body slide up and over the cabin sides. The small
porthole grew blacker and Mossey knew that only the thickness
of the glass separated him from the beast. The sides of the cabin
creaked as pressure was exerted. How frail and fragile the poor
wooden structure seemed that so recently had embodied all the
security and comfort of a home. It seemed that the creature would
crush it as easily as Mossey could crush an empty matchbox in his
hand. Did the thing know he was there? Had it come for him after
. . . after . . . but Mossey couldn't finish the thought. His trous-

ers were again wet and he messed himself as the terror gripped him. The teapot fell from his grasp and the scalding tea spilled itself over his boots. He crouched low on the side bed drooling and gibbering, waiting for the wooden structure to collapse, waiting for the final horror of his appalling end. The fire dimmed and smouldered through the hours but Mossey had lost all impetus to add more coal; perhaps the warmth from the fire had attracted the creature back from its hole. He crouched there, listening but not hearing, watching but seeing nothing, only the darkend circle of the porthole. Gradually the pressure loosened and, after what seemed to be interminable hours, he thought it had gone away.

They found him the next day when it was reported that the *Juniper* had not arrived at Stone for offloading. Mr Jones had reported the wave which had poured back through the tunnel and out over the towpath but it didn't seem very significant at the time. Mr Skinner would report at the other end what had happened. Jones wasn't really concerned and he was in a hurry to be off. The wave had stopped the pump from working but he could see to that in the morning. If there had been a fall Skinner could always back out; only three-quarters of a mile either way; nothing. In those days lives were easily expendable and no one treated the casualties very seriously.

So it was the next morning before a search party from either end was organized. The boats carried lights and pickaxes and a dozen men. The *Juniper* was jammed hard up against a pile of rubble and there was a gash in the side wall which seemed, on first inspection, to break through into some of the mine workings which led off from the earlier tunnel.

The cabin doors were bolted and, however much they shouted and banged, they could get no reply.

"Bugger," said one of the men who had got out onto the towpath. "Look at the sodding state of the boat. Let's get the bugger out of here." They fixed a couple of straps to the stern of the *Juniper* and dragged it back into the daylight. Horrified they looked at the shredded canvas sheets, the salt bags slit and gnawed and the salt defiled by a million droppings.

"Mr Skinner, Mr Skinner. Open up. We've got you out. Open up."

One man with a pickaxe let fly at the wooden doors of the cabin and splintered them. A couple of the pink, hairless rats leapt past them and back into the darkness of the tunnel. "See that?" said Joe with the pickaxe. "Must 'a bin 'undreds o' the buggers to 'a done all this."

They found Mossey still crouched on the side bed, stinking and quite insensible. Of Mr Skinner there was no sign and no one volunteered to return to look for him. The tunnel was a danger-ous place; there could be another fall. They had done what they could and Mr Skinner had obviously been crushed by the rocks; nothing further they could do.

Mossey recovered but was hopelessly deranged; not violent or difficult, but terrified at being left alone and utterly crazed of the dark. He'd not open a door if it was dark outside and if left alone would sit for hours crouched on his haunches, head hidden in his arms.

Mrs Aston offered to look after him. He seemed to trust her and followed her round like a dog. It was said that she had to take him to bed with her in order to get a night's rest herself. She per-suaded him to sign some necessary papers about Skinny's prop-erty. She sold the house in Middlewich and with the money from that together with the money Skinny had left in the bank she bought annuities for herself and Mossey. It seemed a fair enough deal to all concerned.

After a while she encouraged him to sit in the bar and to drink the gin which he could afford to buy on the money she allowed him. They all knew old Mossey and his terrors. DTs a lot of them said, those who didn't remember or who hadn't heard the story of the fall in the tunnel. Mossey's speech had become thick and inarticulate, but Mrs Aston understood him well enough. She was the only person who had some notion of the horrors Mossey had lived through that night. From his ravings on the bad nights, his crazed fear of the dark and his jerks of terror at any scratching or rasping sound, she vaguely understood what had happened to Mr Skinner. But she had his money. A brief will held by the bank clearly stated that she and Mossey were the legal beneficiaries and when it became obvious that Mr Skinner was no longer alive the money was hers. She had taken care of Mossey as her share of the bargain. Mrs Aston was very fair in her dealings. It was a pity it was this way but it couldn't be helped. There were times when she had admitted to herself that it was unlikely Mr Skinner would have married her. Perhaps, for her, things had turned out for the best.

The tunnel was closed indefinitely for repairs. It was thought that the rats could be disease carriers and, as funds were short, repairs were delayed until long after Mossey and Mr Skinner were forgotten . . .

Never Tie Up Under the Spinneys

An evening of telly, thought Liz as she put the completed story back in the shoe box. There was usually a play on at this time. The after-images from her own story would fuse and be lost in her absorption with the efforts from another's pen; or so she hoped.

She fiddled with the aerial but all she could get was a very distorted picture. The sound, too, was uncertain, barely audible. Trees, and the wind in the trees; too late now to make the effort of moving the boat. She tried the radio; nothing again, but that was hardly surprising. It was a very old model which had survived a fire; the controls were dodgy and it was always a surprise when

97

she did get a station free from whistles and gratings. This time she was out of luck; probably it needed new batteries.

She opened the side-doors to look out at the darkening night. The roar of traffic on the motorway half a mile distant amplified. Then, across the continuous growl of sound came the rasp of a train which hurled itself through the night on the far side of the trees. "Peace and quiet," thought Liz wryly as she shut the doors on the intruding noise. The near sounds were friendly and familiar; even the light skittering of feet across the cabin roof made her smile with recognition; a bird, out too late for its own good.

The wind was freshening; better check the stakes. She stood on the bank for a while looking through the netted branches at the sky, darker with clouds overhead. There was a feel of rain; how it was needed after the past weeks when the infrequent storms had done nothing to raise the water level in the canal. The lack of rain at this time of the year seemed unnatural, like so many other unnatural happenings and conditions we were imposing upon ourselves. A sleek brown shape sliced through the water from the opposite bank and darted into the grass verge almost at her feet; a water-rat who knew his territory better than any human intruder could hope to do. A pair of ducks, mallard, whirred upstream just skimming the water's surface soon out of sight in the growing dark. Whatever was there to be afraid of, Liz wondered, in this small intimate world of homely sounds? However had the old superstition arisen? Never tie up under the Spinneys. The old fears seemed senseless and without foundation. The real menace seemed to lie in the continuous roar from the motorway, a reminder of the man-made monster with man as the sacrificial offering. The confusion, the filth and the turmoil of 'civilized' living conditions were epitomized for Liz in the motorway. It seemed to crouch like a beast which threatened her ever-retreating world of reality and serenity.

Never tie up within sight or sound of the motorway made better sense to her as it was a constant reminder of an alien way of life which threatened to engulf and destroy all the skitterings and rustlings which filled her own life with such pleasure and companionship. She shuddered with a sense of foreboding for a future where there would be no place for anyone such as herself. In another month or so there would be other juggernauts charging up and down the canal parallel to the motorway; and where would she go then?

Slowly she returned to the warmth and soft light of the cabin and slowly she ate her supper, enjoying the full savour of such precious moments still left to her. Through the uncurtained windows she could see a quarter moon scurrying between the dark cloud shapes; the promise of rain in the air smelt good. She busied herself with all the unimportant jobs which occupied much of her time and then sat down to write up her diary, the habit of a lifetime. She thought nostalgically of the war years when there had been no motorway and when the canal itself had been a highway for transport. What had they been carrying that trip when she had stemmed the boats up on that bend? Was it iron pilings? Or crates of corned beef? Or was it grain? She couldn't remember and couldn't be bothered to check from an ancient copybook in which she had made her sporadic entries at the time. She shrugged herself back to the present and to an awareness that the wind had risen considerably. She'd have to check ropes and stakes yet again so that she would sleep easily.

She listened apprehensively to the crash and creak of branches. "Don't tie up under the Spinneys." Suddenly the phrase was meaningful. She remembered the previous winter when she and Noelle had hacked their way through great networks of branches from trees fallen across the Cut in a gale. To be tied up under the Spinneys in another such gale could be extremely dangerous. She half considered moving the boat down to the shelter of the next bridge but when she looked out it was obvious that such a feat would be impossible. The wind was tearing through the trees, a real westerly gale with spits of rain preluding the storm. She'd have to stay put and pray that her particular seventy feet of the Spinneys would be safe from crashing trees or falling branches.

Finally she went to bed; the boat was snug and hardly moved despite the wind. She had suspended a couple of tyres from the cabin roof to protect the side of the boat from being buffeted against the coping; the stakes were firmly embedded in the bank and the ropes had tautened in the rain. She had slept through many such storms before – but not under the Spinneys, she thought with a slight superstitious shudder. The cat curled up in the small of her back for companionship and she was glad of his presence. All hell seemed to be let loose outside; not even the sound of distant traffic could be heard above the elemental sound of the force eight gale – or maybe a force ten, she wondered. An ominous clattering and banging across the roof meant that the tin from the exhaust pipe had blown off; a less definable rush of another object left her wondering whether it was the mop or one of the smaller bags of coal; she hoped that the chimneys would hold. Gradually all sounds, resolved themselves into the continuous roar of the wind and Liz dozed fitfully.

Suddenly she was wakened by a great tearing and rending sound. She had a flash-back to the time when a doodlebug had stopped its halting flight right over her flat and she had buried her head under the pillow, waiting. Instinctively she buried her head again – waiting.

In the morning the sun was shining through the curtains. A great peace, like very early Sunday mornings, pervaded the cabin from the outside and Liz lay there wondering at the complete transition from the fury of the storm to the quiet serenity of the morning sun. She listened to the rustlings and scutterings on the bank outside the open hopper window and felt reassured by the sound of familiar scrapings on the roof which indicated that the long, green expanse had attracted a couple of birds, starlings by the noise they were making. The cat had gone and Liz hoped they wouldn't be over-confident in their courtship dance or whatever it was they were up to with their chattering and sudden little flurries of claws and wings.

She lay there listening and identifying all the small distinct sounds of the morning. Gradually she became aware that something was missing; puzzled, she thought over her 'territory' where she had moored the previous day. There was no movement of the boat and it still seemed to be securely tied in the same place; the slight creak of branches nearby recalled the fury of the previous night. There was a pervading stillness which made her feel slightly uneasy. Suddenly she realized what it was that was missing; there was no background roar from the motorway. The chitterings and rustlings, the brushings and scratchings amongst the grass and trees were against a backdrop of silence. There was no continuous or even sporadic roar; not even the steep swoop of a plane which was usual, especially on a Sunday as the flight path followed the canal along this stretch and Sunday so often seemed to be chosen by the RAF for dawn practice flights. Liz listened for the sound of a train; the inter-city line was busy most days, even on Sundays; but however long she listened – and she seemed to have been listening for the best part of an hour – there was no sound of any train rushing past beyond the trees. She was puzzled, but continued to lie there enjoying the peace and quiet of the morning. She thought it was Sunday but couldn't remember for sure; days came and went on the canal and she often lost count of them. It didn't matter; she was content to lie there and enjoy the present. The respite wouldn't last long; she'd make the most of it. As the silence continued she began to speculate on the possible cause. There had been a bad pile-up and traffic had been diverted; the storm had smashed electricity cables; whatever the cause the continued silence seemed uncanny and Liz grew uneasy.

"Better get up and investigate," she thought. "Time I was up anyway – wonder where Simmy is – he's usually around demanding to be fed."

Her usual roll-over-and-out didn't happen. She *thought* she had rolled over, but when it came to groping for her slippers she most certainly had *not* rolled over. She was still on her back looking at the golden planks of the roof timbers. She could visualize in her mind what she wanted to do but her body stayed where it was. Thoroughly frightened she concentrated all her will and effort to turn over again and roll out of the bed. It was no good; she was precisely where she had been and, in a moment of sheer panic, realized that no effort she could make would get her anywhere else.

"My God, I'm paralysed," she thought frantically, "paralysed totally and completely. Must have had a blow in the night and not realized it; or maybe I've had a stroke – a thrombosis – what else?"

She lay there submerged in the continuous waves of panic and fear which threatened to overwhelm her.

"Will anyone find me? Shall I never walk again? What will happen to me? I'd sooner be dead."

Disjointed phrases of horror and self-pity flowed through her. Very gradually she calmed a little.

"Should be thankful to be alive I suppose." But then she wasn't so sure. Young people re-adjusted to life in a wheel-chair; she was too independent, too used to the freedom of her own way of life.

Better to be dead; she'd never re-adjust to being helpless and dependent.

How badly was she paralysed? She felt too terrified to explore the responses of her body immediately. Her spine must be broken; she had not been able to turn over. Perhaps her arms and hands were unaffected but she delayed the effort of trying to move them. She could see; the cabin was still her cabin with the half-open wardrobe at the end of the bed. The wooden carving of an old African traveller stood solidly on the shelf; everything was as it should be as far as she could see. But could she really see? Or was she just 'seeing' it all in her mind because she knew it all so intimately? She blinked to make sure, or thought she blinked; she couldn't be certain. She could 'hear' the sounds on the bank; but did she really hear them or were they imprints from past know-ledge and experience? The panic welled up in her all over again and she tried to concentrate will and effort to listen, to hear a sound and to name it.

"I know what's going on out there," she thought. "I'm aware of everything, of the tree branches brushing together, of the birds' claws on the roof, even the barely perceptible lapping of the water against the hull."

Although she was aware of the sounds and of the familiarity of her cabin she couldn't be exactly sure that she was, in reality, actually seeing and hearing it all. Was there a difference she began to wonder?

A small trickle of courage oozed back into her: "I can at least think, I'm conscious of my predicament." This gave her some small degree of comfort. She'd try her hands; her fingers seemed to feel the fabric of the duvet and she could sense the weight of it over her. But the fingers wouldn't move. She tried desperately to lift an arm to flick back the curtain; if only she could glimpse the reality of the branches and the bank to reassure herself that she really was here in the boat where she had eaten her supper the previous evening and had gone to bed while the storm blew about her. Her arm movement was etched clearly in her mind and she was almost convinced she had succeeded in feeling the solidity of the cabin wall and was about to flick back the curtain when the fact that nothing at all had happened struck her consciousness like a death blow. The nervous system must be badly damaged. With the full realization of her complete paralysis she grew coldly calm and began to analyse her situation within the limitations of her knowledge. There would be a break in a vital part of the nervous system *but* she was still able to think, therefore the brain cells were not seriously affected. She could still 'feel'; her emotional response to the situation left her in no doubt of that. But what did that all add up to? Merely that she was alive but otherwise quite helpless.

The panic gripped her again; she tried to shout even though she knew it was useless; she tried to turn her head to shut out the unwavering glare of the sun through the curtains. Now she couldn't even close her eyes against the light. She thought that she had been able to blink, but now she wasn't sure. Perhaps she was getting worse; perhaps this was the last stage of consciousness before death itself. This she found she could accept; this would be preferable to any other alternative she could imagine. Was she already dead in the accepted meaning of the word? Could she breathe and was there a heart-beat? Again she concentrated all her awareness in an effort to discover if there was any movement of her chest, any slight sound that might indicate a heart-beat. She tried to exclude all external sounds and to focus the direction of her mind upon the existence of a heart – beat or the sensation of taking a breath, however shallow. She thought she could discern a slight movement in her chest, but then she was equally certain that she had been mistaken. Any heart-beat would be very faint and slow with her body in such a state of inanimation and her breathing would be so shallow that both would be almost impossible to detect without other aids. She gave up.

"I'm not dead," she thought. "Of that I'm certain. I think, therefore I am. But also I don't seem to be too much alive, whatever that might mean. If I'm found how will anyone know that I *am* alive if I can make no response to indicate that I am? How can I possibly convey that I can still think and register impressions although I can make no recognizable response?"

No doubt there were machines and techniques to detect her peculiar state of consciousness, but suppose she were only cursorily examined by a busy GP anxious to give his time to the more obviously living patients in his practice. Frightful stories of being buried alive flashed through Liz's fertile imagination; even more frightening imaginings of her brain being kept alive in a glass jar attached to a kind of robot body began to torment her. She started to pray for unconsciousness, for death, for *real* death, or not to be found, or anything that would save her from the horrific experiments that her wild imaginings were conjuring up for her poor helpless body.

Her thoughts wandered on; it would have been merciful if her mind could have been as paralysed as her body. Perhaps she *was* dead. How could one know? Perhaps indeed the conscious mind lived on when the body died; in that case she could well be dead. Was she then still bound by her helpless body and the material limits of her cabin? It was certainly so at the moment. She could imagine the trees and the bank, but only because she had seen them the previous day. She could in no way escape from the confines of the cabin although she tried. She thought of the sect of mystical meditators who claim to be able to move out from the confines of the body. She would concentrate all her will to move out from this passive and inert shell, to stand apart from it in order to see it as the mere casing for her real 'self'. She tried, and goodness knows, there were no physical interruptions or distractions to deflect the concentration of her efforts, but nothing happened; no doubt her technique was faulty or else the process was only possible after a novitiate of many years.

"Not even a blessed ghost," she thought. "That, at least, would offer scope for some fun. I'm nothing but a mind entombed within a corpse. I can't even decide whether I'm warm or cold." Well, she had at last crystallized her situation in words – she knew the worst. Perhaps this was a stage of death and she would have to wait for a final release from this body on the bed. Spirits were supposed to haunt places where they had lived; some strong emotional tie kept them earthbound, or so she had heard. Would she haunt the *Cetus*? She could have laughed at the thought, if only she could have laughed . . .

Where was the cat? She suddenly wondered as the random thoughts flickered through her mind. He was usually around to hurry her out of bed; but there was no sound or sight of Simmy. She thought miserably of sinking ships – but that was 'rats' not 'cats'. She registered that she could still 'feel' wretched. Surely ghosts didn't suffer from emotions, or did they? They were supposed to feel vengeance and hatred, love too if the truth were known. It was an emotional, not a rational bond which held them to their past existences. Perhaps she would have to wait to be buried before her 'self' could be freed from her body. Black fear possessed her again at the thought of being buried; she'd be buried alive unless there was a sudden metamorphosis before the deed was actually done.

"Why didn't I leave instructions to be cremated?" she thought. "At least to be incinerated would be quick. I could almost bear the thought of that."

Meanwhile she was there, shut away from the fresh morning sun; alive yet not alive, dead and yet not dead. She was left there in a cocoon of existence, wrapped around in the woven shroud of her useless body. It could not be long before she was discovered, an event she both hoped for and feared.

All her rational surmises could not dispel the fear aroused by irrational convictions. "Never tie up in the Spinneys." Is this what the boatmen feared or were there other terrifying experiences which awaited the feckless or the unwary? Liz remembered the urgent haste of Marjorie and Susan to be away from the place, an urgency which was stronger than exhaustion and which drove them to move flat-bottomed boats laden with forty-five tons of steel bars from the suction of the mud-silted bend. Was her rational decision to stay there until energies were refreshed by a night's sleep not rational at all but an irrational act of bravado? It might seem so now that she had deliberately chosen to prove the falsity of belief and custom and superstition, to set herself up against the power of accepted associations and feelings and intuitions inherited by generations. It might seem that she had to prove it the hard way, for herself directly, rather than through the half-told tales and uncertain reputations. Well, now she knew. Given the chance she'd never again tie up under the Spinneys – given the chance.

She lay there speculating upon the folly of her gesture, still hoping, despite the implications, for a footfall on the boat, the sound of a voice, the scrape of a cat's paw at the door of the cabin. She thought of eating, but felt no sensation of hunger. It was as if she were in a deep-freeze with succeeding waves of hope, apprehension, regret, fear, panic, resignation, even curiosity washing through her like the sea waves, filling and ebbing from the clean blanched skeleton of a sheep she had once seen in a deserted cove under the cliffs. Scenes of her life flickered randomly and fitfully as if she were watching slides projected upon a screen. "Like someone drowning," she thought. "If only I could see Noelle." But she was grown up and about her own affairs. Would she wonder why her mother hadn't written? Not for some time, her own fault, her letter writing was as unpredictable as her movements. It would take time for her to become anxious about her. What *would* happen next? Someone must pass this way eventually. *Someone* would begin to wonder at her prolonged absence; but when she was found, what then? And the panic would start all over again; better not to be found perhaps.

The golden day wore on; it seemed a long day for November. Then, as she thought more carefully about it, there were patterns of leafy branches on the shadows through the curtains. It couldn't be November.

Liz experienced yet another shock; this was even worse, as the shadows of the leaves indicated a passing of time. How long was beyond guessing, but it was a long time, too long for a body to have been left there without decomposing; too long, too long.

She thought now without feeling, without fear, without panic. The continued silence in a world which she knew to be full of noise and harsh, intruding sounds was also unnatural and reenforced her reflection that she must indeed be dead.

"I *must* be dead." She continued to reflect upon this strange state of being dead. "I must be dead and this body is not real. I only think it is there hidden under the quilt. Senses are illusory and this impression of a body is only there because I need to have a body, because I expect it to be there. What, in fact, can I really see of myself? Nothing. My eyes, or what I think are my eyes, cannot focus on any part of myself, not even my nose. I feel as if I am there on the bed, under the quilt but, now I really think about it, there is no sensation in my fingers and no real concrete sense of my body's existence. How then do I know that I am here?" She couldn't begin to imagine . . .

"That old boat's still there, tied up. A wonder the ropes still hold."

A man's voice, at last; but what did he mean by "that old boat"? The *Cetus* wasn't exactly new but it was very far from being old. She had lapsed into a state of abstraction; the questions posed by

her problems gave no answers and her mind was tired from her efforts at speculation. The voice roused her from the inertia into which she had fallen; the sound of a voice relit a spark of hope in her; she'd be found at last. The water carried the voice easily through the open part of the hopper window.

"A good place for fish here," said a second voice, lighter and with a slight hesitancy. "The S'Spinneys was always the best place hereabouts."

They stopped and Liz heard the soft dump of a basket on the towpath.

"Good fish anywhere along this stretch since all the powered boats were taken off," said the first voice, an older man by the tone. "But I reckon we'll stay here in the shade. Bit hot for me this time of year."

"Funny they haven't taken the old boat f'from here," said the younger man. "Been here ever since the s'storm, hasn't it?"

"Well, it's no harm to anyone here and I guess there was nowhere to put it. The marinas are all clogged up with boats and it was easier to leave the old thing here. Plenty of others in the same state up and down the Cut."

"S'seems a pity. Must have been quite a good boat once."

There were sounds of settling; a camp stool creaked on being opened; the reel of a line was wound and there were soft footfalls on the grass. Liz strained to catch every movement and prayed they would continue to talk although she knew that serious fishermen did not talk.

The settling down preparations continued and Liz could imagine the slow methodical movements of both men from the small sounds across the narrow strip of water. If only they'd keep talking.

"Brought anything to drink, Harry?"

"What do you think?" and Harry laughed shortly. "Here, have a swig before we get too busy."

"Good s'stuff. What's in it?"

"Strong tea well laced. Best recipe I ever met with for fishing. Jo's coming down later with some supper. Said she'd bring some for you too, Jim, as she guessed you'd not think about it."

"Nice of her," said Jim. "It's a bit far to come though, isn't it?"

"Not when she's with Marty. He's out from town for a few

days' holiday. Good walk will do him good."

Harry sounded an easy-going, cheerful sort of character. Was Jo his daughter, Liz wondered.

"L'let's get down to it then." Perhaps Jim wanted to get in some serious fishing before the arrival of Jo and Marty.

There followed a long agony of waiting. How Liz longed to sit up and bang at the window, to have them notice her, include her in their pleasantries. She longed just to hear their voices again, but the serious business of fishing had overtaken them. The occasional fishing talk of "got one there", "too small to keep" followed by a faint plop, and "careful now or you'll lose him" was all that she could hear. Resigned to her fate, condition or state in which she found herself Liz took pleasure in feeling again the proximity of her own kind. They were hard, fickle, unimaginative, irresponsible, insensitive, unpredictable, overtly serious about trivialities and casually indifferent to the real issues which directed their life styles; lightened sometimes by streaks of strange humour; unreliably honest when it suited their immediate purposes, but blandly dishonest and careless about fundamentals such as sincerity and truth in their dealings and relationships. Yet she was one of them and closer to those two men stubbornly sitting through the summer evening than to the predictable fussy little squirrel chittering its anxiety over the invasion of its territory. She could see them in her mind as clearly as if she were sitting on the bows of her boat watching them. Each movement, however slight, came clearly across the water to her, accentuated by the absence of all other sound. That was still a mystery too; the roar from the motorway was still absent. There should be the sound of an occasional train; she must have forgotten to notice them passing in the obsession with her own dilemma; but as time went by she noted that there was no sound of either a train or an overhead aeroplane. All transport had ceased. There must have been a major disaster of which she had been a victim whereas the fishermen had escaped. If only she could get up, catch their attention somehow, ask them just one simple question, and the mystery would be solved. She might even be glad to be dead rather than alive, if indeed to be dead meant that she could still be aware of all that was happening around her. It would be nice to move though; perhaps that came later.

"Here they come," said Harry. "Across the bridge over there. About time too, I'm starved."

"Took their time on th'the way I guess," said Jim. "It's a tidy long walk though."

"Different from the old days when we used to whip down here in the old Bedford van."

"I like it this way now I'm used to it," said Jim. "Quieter and easier, specially for us in the country."

"There wasn't much country left; not real country; but it's coming back. Takes time," Harry commented.

"Take fishing now," continued Jim who lost his hesitancy as he talked. "I used to chuck 'em back again. No use keeping what I didn't use. And all those competitions; rows and rows of us, all serious stuff. Couldn't stop to talk or to have a bite; might miss the big 'un that'ud get you the silver cup. Kids' stuff really when you think about it. Nowadays I take back all I can catch and sell it in town; sell it for food, real food. What's more, there's plenty of fish now, good fish, roach and perch and even bream which makes good eating. They'd all but finished any real fishing before the fuel cut."

"Go on, go on," thought Liz. "Perhaps that's it. Oil supplies cut off. Could be worse."

Jim's comments were cut short by the arrival of two others; the young couple with the supper, Liz guessed.

"Hallo you two, caught much?" A young, bright, female voice tripped nearer. "One hell of a way to get here, even by the short-cut. Took us over an hour, didn't it Marty?"

"Sure did," replied a town voice, clipped with a faint Cockney twang.

"Not so far as you'll have to walk before your holiday's over," said Harry. Their voices were all so different, so individual, that Liz had no difficulty in recognizing their owners. She could almost 'see' each one of them: Harry, middle-aged, square and solid, capable-looking; Jim, younger, thin and countrified, but with a kindly sensitive face, shy with strangers, warm and dependable with his few friends; the girl, young and leggy, lively and energetic, in jeans and pullover like so many of her generation; Marty was less distinct in her mind, a 'towny', sure of himself, slightly patronizing to the country-folk.

"I don't mind the walking," he said, "if only I'd got some

proper boots. 'These shoes ain't made for walking'," he intoned.

"Take them off and go barefoot like me," laughed the girl. "Soon get used to it."

"All this back-to-nature stuff," he grumbled, but Liz could tell he was only repeating what everyone else was probably saying. No one ever agreed with changes. People re-adapted their living patterns remarkably easily but continued a kind of plainsong of complaint and resentment about the change itself. Perhaps this was the only gesture they could make about decisions which they felt powerless to influence.

Liz had heard it all before. She felt that she could almost predict the responses of one of the group to the others. She wondered why she found it so easy to imagine them all so clearly. Were they only imprints from her past existence? Were they really out there talking together or was this a scene from a flash-back of memory? No, that wasn't possible; the reference to the fuel cut divorced the present from any past she had known. Yet the characters seemed familiar, or were they? So many human beings fell into recogniz-able groups despite the small individual tricks of speech and habits of movement, appearance and behaviour. Without doubt she had known other Harrys, Jims, Martys; if only she could recall just one of them in sufficient detail to give him a name that would be meaningful to her. She seemed to remember and identify her daughter; the girl on the bank had a similar way of talking, but all that generation seemed to affect the brightly casual, slightly hard way of teasing and passing confident opin-ions. "I am sure that I don't know any of them," Liz thought. "And this is a present of which I am a part, but only as an inanimate spectator."

As if to confirm her thoughts the young girl's voice again broke in upon her consciousness.

"Why have you chosen to sit opposite that old boat, Dad?" she said. "It's quite spooky. Plenty of room farther up the bank."

"Good fish on this stretch under the trees," said Harry. "Fish like shelter, roots and shadows. Bet some of them find that old boat a good hiding place."

"What's it doing here?" Liz heard the young man say. What was his name? Marty? Short for Matthew, Martin? "Thought they'd all been cleared off a couple of years ago."

"Well, mostly all the powered boats were in the marinas when

111

the Cut came. They'd been warned of course. But this one had been caught in a gale and it was pretty badly smashed up. You can see how the front of the boat is all stove in. An old girl used to live aboard – used to see her sometimes on this stretch. Either she didn't know what was coming or she ignored the warnings, or, more likely, got caught in the gale just before it all happened."

"What happened to her then?" asked the girl.

Liz's attention was riveted; answers at last. "Found by a fisherman," continued Harry. "Not one of us; one of those who used to come out by car and still kept coming even when he had to walk from town. Pretty bad she was. Took her off to hospital. Don't know what happened. Died most likely."

"So it's true," thought Liz. "I am dead. Then how do I come to be here? Is this my 'territory' where I must stay until I am released? If one ever is released. Well, it could be worse." Better than getting marooned in a poky bed-sit in town where she had once been advised to spend her declining years. So dangerous for her alone on the boat everyone said. The gale, the Spinneys, the crash on the boat; that all made sense. If only she had been properly nervous as Jan and Steph had been in the old days, if only she had been sensible and returned to a proper mooring, if only . . . But what else had happened? Something to do with oil supplies; there had been some scare about limiting supplies for essential services but no one she knew had taken it more seriously than to stock up with a few spare gallons. Whatever had happened since the gale, the results seemed to be pretty radical and extensive. If only Harry and Jim, Marty and the girl would talk some more about the strangeness of the situation; but, she reflected, it was no longer strange to them. Had one of them said something about two years? Had she really been encapsulated here for that long? How was it possible? The talk on the bank dwindled to trivialities of the fish they had caught, the sandwiches, the weather; and Liz's attention drifted. She felt removed from them as if already she was in a different state of consciousness than they were. What did it matter what had happened? It couldn't affect her now. She was sorry about the boat though. The *Cetus* had been a good boat; pity the gale had made such a mess of the front cabin. Had Simmy been killed too, she wondered, or had he escaped to live wild?

"Come on, Marty. I'm going over to have a look at the boat."

The words brought Liz back to the people on the bank. The girl was coming over and persuading the young man to join her.

"Come and have a look at the engine then," she wheedled. "Bet it's all rusted up. Come *on*. I'm scared to go by myself but I want to have a look."

"They're coming," thought Liz, "and I can't do anything about it. Will they know I'm here I wonder?"

She heard the crunch of dead, dry twigs and felt the two of them close by on the bank. She could sense their nearness.

"See anything?" shouted Harry.

"It's a dreadful mess," shouted back the girl. "What a shame."

"Looks as if it will fall apart any minute," said Marty. "Look at this old engine-room. An old Lister, air-cooled, I think. Good engines in their day."

Liz bridled. It *was* a good engine, strong and reliable; never let her down in all the time she had travelled the canals.

"Why on earth don't they get it moved? It's a real eyesore. Spooky too. Wouldn't surprise me if the old girl doesn't still haunt it," said the girl.

"Little does she know," thought Liz.

"Don't be daft. It would fall to pieces if it were moved; and then, what a business it would be to get it out. Best left alone I'd say. Come on, let's see if we can steal a look into the cabin while we're here. Maybe there're some old horse brasses."

"Marty King, you're dreadful. You've no morals. Fancy thinking of helping yourself. You'll be cursed if you do. Those old boat people didn't much like people such as you." She giggled and Liz could feel the boat move slightly under the weight of a foothold.

"Been rifled long ago by the looks of it," shouted Marty, his voice muffled.

"Must have got into the cabin," thought Liz.

"Nothing here. Wonder if there's anything in the back cabin though. It's sealed off; can't get in. Must have been where it was struck."

"Can't see anything," said the girl, almost directly level with Liz's head. "Curtains are all in rags but still across the window and the window's closed this side. Dark in there . . . Oh my God!" she screamed.

"What the hell was that?" shouted Marty.

"What's wrong? You all right?" came at the same time from across the water.

"Marty," the girl was gibbering. "Marty, did you see it?"

The boat lurched as Marty jumped off to join her.

"Yes, I thought I did," he said. "What the hell was it? A rat?"

"Look, there it is, up there in the tree, right high up."

"My God, it's a cat. A black and white cat. Must have been hiding there in the wreckage."

Liz was shaken. Simmy hadn't deserted after all. How on earth had he survived? Then she remembered the rabbits he used to catch and smiled to herself – if that had been possible.

"Let's get out of here," the girl's voice was hard. "I told you it was spooky."

"That cat's real enough," said Marty, "though a bit wild by the look of him."

"Poor Simmy," Liz thought, "he'll be scared. Could do with a good home."

"It's only a cat," shouted Jim. "Can s'see it from here. Poor thing's s'scared."

"Must be a wild one," said Harry. "Holed up in the old boat for cover."

The young couple had moved away, probably to rejoin the fishermen.

"I did hear the old woman had a cat," remarked Harry as the young couple came along the towpath. "Wonder if it could be the same."

"After all this time?" said Jim. "How long is it since we went off oil? Two years is it? Not possible a cat would survive so long."

"Could be," replied Harry. "Cats are canny creatures at survival," and Liz's heart warmed to him.

"Poor puss," said Jim after a pause, while Liz wondered what Simmy's fate eventually would be. "Tell you what, Harry. Think I'll stay on for a bit to see if it comes down. Don't like to think of it deserted."

"You've always been a bit soft about animals," said the girl. "Don't fancy your luck with this one though. What'll you do with it supposing you *do* manage to catch it? Looks completely wild to me."

"I could do with a cat. Since young Ginger got caught in a rabbit wire I haven't fancied another. This one now, he'd have more sense than to get himself caught. I'll hang on anyhow until the ferry boat's gone up. Shouldn't be long now."

Liz could hear him call the cat. A sigh, or the semblance of a sigh, went through her. Poor, faithful Simmy, he'd be much better off with Jim than staying around dead memories. Poor old *Cetus*, so that was it, no oil supplies for some reason or another. Poor old boat, poor old puss, poor Liz. How sad . . . how sad . . .

Her thoughts drifted in and out of focus while the young couple continued their speculations upon the fate of the boat and herself.

"Couldn't get into the back cabin at all. The door seems to have jammed. Could have shoved it though if that damned cat hadn't scared Jo out of her wits."

"Best leave it alone," said an older voice.

"Wonder the windows haven't all been smashed. Looks as if someone has been inside. No sign of any belongings."

"The young hooligans keep to the towns – nothing much out here to tempt them. I think the old girl had a daughter or someone who would have taken anything of use."

"The engine's still there – pity to let it rust like that."

"No good to anyone these days."

"Good for scrap – should fetch a quid or two."

"And who's going to the trouble of lifting it out?'

"Wonder why the back cabin is blocked off? The window on the bank side is shut tightly too, but the one on this side is open."

"Better swim over then."

"We could go back and peer over from the cabin top."

"Wouldn't see much, still some curtains across."

"Perhaps I could pull them back a bit."

"Time's getting on. Isn't that the ferry boat? We'll have to move out of its way."

"Tell you what, Jo. We'll come back in daylight and have a proper look at the boat if you're that interested."

"Best leave it be," cautioned the older voice. "You could be done for trespassing. Still quite a few folk around and I guess that Jim Coles and his son keep an eye on it. Lock-keeper and lengthman on this stretch," he explained.

"Quite a few working boats back again now. Horses fetching q'quite a price."

"Here's the ferry boat now. Wish it were going the other way. I'd cadge a lift."

"Where to, stupid?" said the girl.

"Anywhere just so's I don't have to walk," he laughed. "Come on then. Better get going before I change my mind and cadge a lift up to the pub. I'll carry your basket, Dad."

"Nice old horse. I bet he'll be glad of his s'stable tonight."

Liz felt a slight movement of the *Cetus* in the bow wave of an oncoming boat. No sound of an engine, only the soft thud of horse hooves on the further bank. Sadly, the voices receded down the towpath. They would be on the lane over the bridge, leaning over to watch the progress of the boat beneath them.

"Tie up along here for a drink," shouted a strong young voice.

"Old Arthur could do with a bit of a rest before the last lap."

"Okay. Just beyond that old boat," another voice replied from what Liz imagined must be the bows of the oncoming boat. There were other voices and someone was singing a Harry Lauder song, 'Roamin' in the Gloamin'' with others trying to join in. The voices of the fishermen were now quite lost in the growing sounds from the ferry boat. Or perhaps they had now moved away, back to the comfort of their homes. Liz wondered if Jim had been serious in trying to get hold of Simmy. He'd not have much chance with this new invasion.

"Stop the horse," shouted the second voice. "This is the only place we can get right in along here. I'll see if Annie is ready with the drinks and sandwiches."

They were stopping, right here under the Spinneys. Were they mad? Didn't they realize the danger? Anything could happen here after dark and it was almost dark now. Liz heard them laughing and joking; caught snatches of talk from the boat which was now tied up on the towpath side just beyond the *Cetus*. Didn't they know? Hadn't they heard about the Spinneys?

Never tie up under the Spinneys . . . Never tie up under the Spinneys. She was desperate to communicate the danger to them . . . "Don't tie up . . . don't tie up . . ."

A sharp voice cut through across her struggling efforts, "Liz . . . Liz . . . all right, it's all right. You're back, you're all right . . . Liz."

The voice was insistent, penetrating, demanding. It seemed to reach through to some deep part of her that was struggling to reach the surface, demanding of her to make some effort before it was too late.

"She's coming back. She's coming."

With a final desperate effort Liz opened her eyes and was certain this time that she really *had* opened them, had obeyed the direction from the insistent voice which had cut through her fears for the boat tied up under the Spinneys. Faces were smiling at her, faces she dimly recognized. The room was small and clean and light.

"Simmy," she said and heard herself say it.

"He's all right," said a bright young voice; it sounded like the girl on the bank. "I've got him home with Steph, waiting."

"Don't tie up," gasped Liz closing her eyes again; the light was very bright after the gloom of the cabin.

"We know," said another voice. "Don't tie up under the Spinneys, especially after nightfall. You've been trying to tell us for the past week."

"She'll be all right now. Let her sleep," said the authoritative voice.

The Anchorage

Liz recovered, slowly at first; she was a bad patient and left the hospital before the doctor gave permission; concussion needed weeks, months of care and supervision and Liz was to regret her impatience to be up and around. She stayed with Steph, but the innumerable cats and the untidiness soon began to irritate. The headaches with which she was now afflicted made her over-susceptible to movement as well as to noise. She knew that she should have remained the extra two months in the hospital but would not admit it, refused to return even when the doctor made the suggestion.

The boat had been damaged beyond repair but luckily it had been well insured. There would be just enough money to buy that cottage which she had once considered vaguely as a possibility. Noelle was now working as a health visitor, enjoying the work and with no regrets about the change of career. She came often to the cottage, knew that Liz was irritable too often for comfort and for her own well-being.

"There's a bungalow for sale, not far from the canal – handy for my area," she said. "Would you share it with me, Liz? You could have your own separate rooms; we could even make a second kitchen if you like. It's set back from a quiet by-road. I haven't any cash for a deposit."

"So that's it," laughed Steph. "The insurance money." The 'family discusses', as she called them, always seemed to take place in her cottage, but she was relieved that Noelle had at least made a positive suggestion. Liz could not stay at the cottage for much longer.

"It's a suggestion, that's all." Noelle hoped that Liz wouldn't seriously think of her as mercenary.

Liz agreed thankfully; it seemed to be a good solution for both of them. She wanted to be away from the cottage but had felt unable to make a decision, to face the prospect of arrangements, even of living again her solitary existence. Suddenly Noelle was the stronger, the more capable, the organizer; and Liz was content for it to be so.

"We have your story of the tunnel safe and sound," Steph had told her. "Still on the table where you had left it. What a horror story though. And what about those notes for the 'Jane Story'?" Not yet; her head still throbbed and although she rested every afternoon she didn't want to be bothered with plans, with writing, with people.

Noelle understood her mother's moods and irritability better than Steph and had completed the purchase of the bungalow as speedily as possible; there was only the need for a small mortgage and that had presented no problem. There was enough money for the basic furnishings; as Liz grew stronger she'd be able to buy the extras, it would give her something to do. Noelle completed all the arrangements and in a few weeks Liz felt strong enough to make the move. Noelle had a small car, bought on a loan from the LEA as she needed one for her work. Steph watched them go with a mixture of regret and relief. Liz had been growing ever more irritable, despite the headaches or because of them. She'd be better in her own place.

Jan came for a brief visit to see the bungalow and to reassure herself that Liz was recovered. She approved of the bungalow, its convenient layout and all the gadgets.

"Much more sensible for you in your old age than that boat." Jan had always emphasized the eight years' difference between them. She approved too of Noelle although not of her change of career.

"Poorly paid, welfare workers," she had censored. "Better off as a teacher; shorter hours and longer holidays. Still, as long as you're happy." She mitigated her disapproval. "How old are you now? Must be getting on for thirty."

"Twenty-seven . . . and why am I not married?" laughed Noelle. "What about you three?" then remembered the almost extinct memory of Patrick. "Well, you know what I mean."

"Three old maids . . ." quoted Jan with a grin. Liz had been out of the room. "Persuade your mother to come and stay," she said. "The change will do her good. Besides, there's someone I want her to meet."

"Later," Noelle had said. "We've only been installed for a couple of months. Give her time."

Two more months passed and a letter from Jan came to renew the invitation. "To convalesce," she wrote, "and there's someone I'd like you to meet. You could be interested."

"Very mysterious," said Noelle. "You'll have to go to find out."

It was autumn again before Liz said casually," I think I should make the effort to see Jan or she'll be offended. And my curiosity still gnaws about that letter."

Jan was delighted to see her. She was still slightly overawed by Liz's extra years and her 'brains' – Jan's explanation of the differences she had felt between Liz and herself in the old days. Steph had told her of the published story and she still kept the old magazine well displayed, open at the article.

They reminisced about past days, about shared experiences, common interests, acquaintances and friends linked by time and circumstance into the patterns of their lives. The flat was warm and Liz felt relaxed, better. A shared meal and coffee well laced oiled the springs of memories and the interchange of comments on the fortunes, misfortunes, tragedies even, of those they had known through all the decades of living now behind them. Inevitably much of the talk was of boats, of incidents and accidents of living and working on the canals – the Cut they called it. They talked of the present, of the success of the Mikron Players as they recreated scenes and songs and characters from the not-so-distant past; not so distant in time but distant enough in customs and life-styles from their own sophisticated comforts.

"Remember that boatman's wedding we saw at Braunston? All the boats decorated and the wedding procession up through the field to the church? Who played the accordion? I've forgotten; forgotten too who was married to whom."

"Weddings now. I heard such a strange story. Remember I said I wanted you to meet someone? It's the friend of a friend, or rather the daughter as her mother is in a home. She – the daughter – was turning out her mother's possessions and found this old diary. My friend Mary was telling me about it. Hannah, the daughter, was dreadfully upset; something to do with her brother and the diary. He was a canal enthusiast in the early days of pleasure boats; lived on his own boat most of the time."

At Jan's instigation Mary had read Steph's story, 'Boats Coming', which Liz had written, and it had occurred to Jan that Liz might be interested in the old diary if she could persuade Hannah to lend it. Liz was intrigued. Could she meet Hannah?

It was easily arranged. Mary was a stout, cheerful old lady; and Hannah was older than Liz had expected. She had two grown-up sons and a husband who still spent much of his life at sea. Jan had arranged a good dinner for the foursome hen-party. They talked generalities, prices, noise, pollution; even theatres and concerts. Like everyone else they had so much in common! Jan told Hannah something of their wartime experiences and said that Liz was interested in the folklore and superstitions which once were prevalent among those who travelled the waterways. And so, eventually, the talk turned to the interest for which the evening had been arranged; Hannah's brother James and his story. She didn't say very much and it was obvious that the story still disturbed her.

"I know that you're interested in my brother's story," she said, "but even after ten years I find it hard to talk about. So I've brought along his diary and a few letters and some sheets of writing which we found in the cabin of his boat. You are welcome to borrow them and I hope that the story can be written. I'd like to read it."

She gave Liz a small attaché case. In it were a large, stiff-covered exercise book, just a couple of letters written to his sister, and three sheets of barely decipherable writing. From these Liz wrote the story – James' story, and, as such, written as Liz hoped he might have told it . . .

The Anchorage had been up for sale for over two years. I had passed it once or twice on my travels northwards and wondered why it hadn't been sold and half-wished I had enough money to make a reasonable bid for it. I could only think that it was in too isolated a position to attract even the most enthusiastic of canal travellers; it was on the towpath side too, which meant that the Waterways Board's mooring restrictions might present problems for keeping a boat there. It was an old canal-side pub with the front lawn, now spattered with sheep droppings and beginning to succumb to outcrops of brambles from the hedges, sweeping down to the canal frontage. I had tied there about three years before when it was still opening for two hours at midday; an enthusiast from Middlewich came over daily to try and keep it going. Curiosity had prompted me to tie up my two-berth 'noddy' boat and explore. That's the best of a small boat; it's possible to stop virtually anywhere and to investigate whatever catches the interest – an old church, a deserted priory or a green expanse of golf course; and I often used to nose into the mud of the reeded banks to watch the antics of moorhens, the swans nesting in the spring and the sharp-eyed heron, himself endlessly watching and hunting.

I'm lazy by nature and, although a hard day's boating can fill me with a pleasurable sense of achievement, at the slightest excuse I tie up and idle the days away. A breeze and I can persuade myself that my light fibreglass boat will be at the mercy of the gale; rain of course provides the perfect excuse for not going – such a problem drying out and so unnecessary to suffer rather than to enjoy my extended holiday. My needs are extremely few and I can survive for weeks, as indeed I do, on my store of tins and packets.

I sucked away at my pipe, looking up at the pub and trying to recapture the scenes of earlier days when it had been properly lived in, when the grass was cropped, the windows opened and perhaps children and puppies sprawled under a watchful eye. Two bedrooms I guessed, a cellar and a wash-house at the back. I'd have a proper look round later on . . . If only I had a few thousand; it was isolated enough even for me. Then I thought of ownership; ownership would mean responsibility, continuous work to keep it in decent condition; and a fixed place where people could come and find me. I didn't have a few thousand anyway and my somewhat casual life-style gave no possible indication that such wealth would ever be mine. However, it was fun to play with the idea knowing that the reality of it was impossible. Articles and short stories and a book that constantly eluded my efforts to complete it just about kept me in tobacco; a small legacy kept me in food and, when I couldn't afford petrol for the outboard, I reverted to the role of mule and towed myself to the next long stopping place. I have a kindly married sister who gives me a room through the three darkest months and I make myself useful by fixing gadgets around the house and by helping to educate a couple of untrained young nephews. My brother-in-law is away at sea for long periods so it works out very conveniently for all concerned. It's the kind of life to which I am completely suited. Responsibilities, duties, routine – all the heavy and worthy words frighten me to death; I am absolutely unfit to meet the demands of any of them. Marriage for me could only be with one of those efficient career women who would wish to go on fulfilling herself and who would be willing to leave me in peaceful sloth; it would hardly be a 'marriage' I suppose, but I'd be willing to give her my name and to enliven her commitments and involvements with tales of my casual 'brief encounters'. I can be very entertaining, so I'm told, but only for brief periods – far too exhausting to live in such close proximity that the orthodox marriage condition seems to require. My sister half agrees with me and, in her more honest moments, says that she has a good marriage because Bill is away for so much of the time which leaves her free to 'do her own thing', which conveniently happens to be portrait painting, mostly in oils; 'conveniently' because there's a spare room which she has converted for her own use; and now that my nephews are confined to school for five blissful hours, five days a week, she is able to daub away in peace; does quite well at it too, and makes more than I manage to do by my writing; but then she is far more dedicated than I, has more application and probably more talent.

These random reflections flickered through my mind as I lay on my bunk smoking through the sultry June day and pleasantly passed the time until I heard the van arrive. I sauntered up the grassed slope to meet mine host – in jeans and shirt – as he unlocked the door.

"Don't know why I bother," he said as he pulled me a pint. The beer tasted cool and dark and well worth the couple of hours' wait.

"No locals at all come here?" I asked.

"No locals to come. The trade was off the Cut; in working days it was a popular stop-over; you know how boatmen liked their drink, made up for the tough hours of going I guess. Not very big you see, but enough for half a dozen to sit round the fire in the cold months and plenty of room outside in the summer. Old Ted from Middlewich used to carry bricks on this stretch and said there was a regular day-trip boat that used to stop here and rest the horses and to fill the customers with drink. Weddings here too I believe. They used to get married in town and then come over here for the celebrations."

"Doesn't Ted come over for old times' sake?" I asked.

"Not him; he doesn't like the place. Can't get him to come though I've asked. Superstitious lot – boat people. A place has only to be empty for a year or so and they've got it haunted and cursed by all kinds of wild tales."

He went on talking as I downed my pint. It was, as he said, a very small bar, the space reduced even more by a great settle which shut out the draughts from the door. The cool, earthy brew warranted a second pint although it would mean prolonging a conversation that, already, was beginning to pall.

"How's the canal trade?" I asked – a rhetorical question.

"Not an easy stopping place," he replied. "Most of the hired boats keep going till they reach the town. Just an occasional regular like yourself."

"Hardly call myself a regular – I very rarely stop here."

"You know what I mean, you don't seem to be in too much of a hurry. You'll be back." He paused and looked at me curiously. "Come from round here, do you?"

I always expect the casual, curious enquiry after the first round of exchanges, so I have the answer ready.

"London," I replied easily. "Do a bit of writing which gives me time off. In-between assignments now." Little did he know – but I always get away with it. If I'd said 'hobo' the response would have been quite different. Being a 'writer' always seems to impress. Extraordinary!

"Care to have a look round," Keith said, evidently impressed. "Might give you some ideas for write-ups on canals."

"Thanks," I replied, "I'd like that. I see you have plenty of traditional painting around."

There was a painted wooden panel above the dingy fireplace and another running the length of the counter. There were the usual roses and primitive scenes of turreted castles, lagoons and willow-plate bridges – no lovers, no bluebirds – and a few casual brush strokes to suggest sailing boats and indiscriminate birds. I didn't find them very interesting; they proliferate now in every pretentious boating centre – endless copies of endless copies.

"Originals," said Keith proudly, lightly running his fingers over the counter surface. "Old Josh did most of them. Just used to get bits of wood from the Cut, dry them out and shape them and then put on the paint. Used to nick the paint from the dock. Dead now of course, but old Ted in Middlewich remembers him. He tells some tales when he's in the mood."

Keith was obviously a canal fanatic and I prepared myself to be bored for another hour with his enthusiastic renditions of old Ted's memories.

"I'll have another pint." It would help; good stuff too.

"Come and draw it yourself," said Keith. I followed him down the narrow stone steps, smooth and hollowed in the centre by years of continuous wear by booted publicans. A cool dark well enveloped us as we left the warmth and sunlight of the bar. It was like walking into the cold shallows of the canal; and the coldness moved steadily up through my limbs as we descended. The earthen floor was packed hard as cement and the two barrels stood against one wall on a couple of empty crates.

"Only two barrels?" I asked, if only to hear the sound of my voice in the cold chill of the cellar.

"No call for more," said Keith, who was occupied with tapping the bung of the second barrel. "This one'll last the rest of the summer I reckon, but I can always bring over more in the van if we get a rush – not much hope of that. I'll take back the empty one today and bring over a replacement later on in the week. I like to keep it a month or two down here before use; seems to lend it a flavour – or perhaps I like to think it does," he laughed.

"Nice and cool," I said with a shiver. "Especially on a day like today." I wanted to get back up those stairs into the sunlight. There was nothing else in the small underground box but cobwebs and a smell of emptiness. A great wave of desolation flooded through me like a dark cloud on an April day. A sense of loss, of ineffable sadness and irremediable despair filled me and a great sigh broke upwards from my heart despite myself.

Keith looked up at me sharply as he handed me the mug and picked up his own from the floor.

"Nothing else down here," he said. "Let's go back up. Easy to become morbid in a place like this."

Returning to the warmth of the bar was like surfacing from some dark and bottomless pool.

"I guess the old place will be boarded up when I leave." Keith's voice had an added edge of briskness. "Drink up and I'll show you the rest of the house before we leave."

I swallowed my pint too quickly to enjoy it. The sadness still dragged in my chest and I only wanted to escape from the place. Keith was determined to show me over and my will is never strong enough to withstand another's enthusiasm. I followed him through into the small living-room behind the bar. The blackened range was rusty and ashes still cluttered the grate and the hearth. A well scrubbed wooden table took the centre of the room and grimy lace curtains effectively screened the small window. Keith unlocked and pushed open the back door which led into a scullery and an outhouse. "Depressing, isn't it?" he said. "Just two small bedrooms. Still, when you think of Shelter and all the homeless it makes you wonder why someone doesn't take it over. Could be a nice little home with some work on it."

"Why don't you take it over?" I thought to myself. "Since you're so bloody keen on tradition and all that."

127

I followed him back into the bar.

"Not for me though," he went on. "I'm off to Liverpool in the autumn. Got a place at the University to read History. After that I might think about it," he added, knowing well that he'd have to be pretty desperate even to consider living here, apart from having to persuade some love-crazed maiden to join him in a back-to-nature undertaking.

"I know what you think," he said defensively. "A canal romantic who backs off from the reality."

"Who owns the place?" I asked.

"The land is owned by Tylers of Mountshay farm and the pub was built by a renegade member of the Wedgewood family – to tempt the boatmen from their sober ways. The Wedgewoods were Quakers you know and he wanted to get back at them."

"Funny way to do it," I observed.

"Drank himself to death. His idea of a joke, I guess. Anyway there's a clause in the deeds which requires it to be used as a 'tavern for boatmen' and it cannot be used for anything else. There's a lease on it; only a few more years to run and then it reverts to the owners of Mountshay. Doesn't seem worth while to have the deeds legally changed. I work for the estate agent who has charge of the property. I'm paid a small fee to come over here. It's good to get out of the office for a couple of hours and I'm a bit cracked on canals too – as if you hadn't noticed." He laughed and the wall of melancholy which had separated me from him gradually dispelled.

"Think I'll finish with a good tot of rum, if you've got it. Then I guess you'll want to be off," I said. The rum should clear the last shades of whatever had overtaken me in the cellar.

"No one else calling in today. Yes, rum it is," said Keith taking a bottle from the shelf behind the bar. "Better do some dusting while you drink – soon gets mucky back here. Beer's the most popular."

As he busied himself with dusting and tidying my eyes wandered over the faded and mildewed wallpaper. It was an old pattern with vertical lines of roses against a background of trellis; a couple of hunting prints seemed vaguely out of place. There was a fine mesh of cobwebs in the enlarged cracks between the shrunken boards of an old butty 'ellum leaning against the wall behind the bar and the yellowed, straggly remains of a horse's tail brushed against the black oblong of the cellar doorway.

"Time's up," said Keith cheerfully. "Must be getting back. Better come again soon," as we moved out into the sunlight, "or maybe there won't be anyone here to open up. Can't think anyone'll take it over when I go." He looked at me squarely as if the idea had suddenly occurred to him although I knew that it had been in his mind for the past hour. "Look here, why don't you take it on? Good place for writing – nice and quiet; good mooring and you only need to unlock at one and lock up again at three. Couldn't be better." He became more enthusiastic as he talked.

"Couldn't be tied though," I said hastily before he should become too serious and persistent in his suggestion. "Also, I don't think BWB would allow a permanent mooring on the towpath side."

"That could soon be fixed – no problem. Just a thought," he said getting into the van. "Mind you, being here nights is different from coming over midday. The place has a bit of a reputation according to Ted; but then, old deserted places usually do, don't they? A bit of atmosphere is good for selling too. Let me know if you change your mind, about taking the job I mean. Here's a card from the firm – Middlewich – and just ask for me, Keith Gravelly," he said writing his name on the back. "Ted says there's bodies buried under the floor of the cellar. Could be, I suppose, but you know how these tales get around," and he slammed into gear and moved off down the track waving a hand out of the window as he went . . . waving a hand.

"Cheerful bloke," I thought, glad to be left alone again. I was exhausted by those two hours and thankfully stretched myself on the bunk in the privacy of my small cabin.

That had been three years ago and, of course, I had done nothing about the job although I often played with the possibility in my mind. I could easily have made the place habitable for my simple needs. There was a good well of water; no electricity but that wouldn't have bothered me; I'm used to candles and a paraffin lamp on the boat. But, like any other serious project I only played with the idea; I really had no intention of becoming so committed. I have passed that stretch only a few times since then to see the windows boarded and sheep using the frontage as an extension of their adjoining field. I haven't tied up there as it

hasn't seemed particularly expedient or suitable to do so. A
shadow of the still remembered wave of sadness tinged me
whenever I idled my time away thinking back on my visit there. I
had no reason to tie up on that deserted frontage and no wish to
do so either. I'm not fond of morbid fancies but, unfortunately,
am only too susceptible to 'suggestions'. Keith's last gem of
information could so well be true; there are so many tales up and
down the Cut of bloody fights and savage murders. A hard life,
hasty tempers and lack of social restraints resulted in a way of life
which fully bore out the fears and suspicions with which the
normal citizen regarded the Cut and the 'bargees' who lived and
worked on it. The canal was a place to be feared and never to be
near after dark so we all kept well away until the boom in holiday
traffic broke up the fears and superstitions associated with the
dark bridges and the still, oily waters. My flights of fancy followed the current trendy image of elegant boats gliding through
well-cared for waterways with marinas and lidos aesthetically
contrived in a landscape of weeping willows and gracious lawns.
Thoughts of the Anchorage kept me rooted in a far more brutal
past. I'd be glad when the lease was up and the place could be
pulled down or put to some more useful purpose than the
harbouring of outworn memories.

However, that all seems so long ago when I was young and free
and unambitious and when clouds over the sun meant only
refreshing storms and showers of rain; when each day stretched
invitingly ahead and the nights were warm and drowsy and
made for loving and sleeping and easy dreams; when I was a
cheerful, easy-going layabout whom people liked, even though
grudgingly, and who enjoyed the casually serious affairs when
the romantically sexy mood would not be denied. The boat
provided the perfect background for my ephemeral romances.
"Come back to my place" and the silly sentimental response to
being taken for a trip to some suitably isolated tie-up in the rushes
or under a willow tree reduced my efforts at seduction to a
minimum. They fell for my charms like hypnotized hens. When
the signals were out that the affair might deepen and become
serious, on the girl's part and very occasionally on my own, I'd be
away and settle back into my more comfortable bachelor habits in
a further part of the waterways network. I kept memos in my
diary of the pub or the theatre where I had met Louise or Anne or

Sarah so that I'd keep clear for the next year or so by which time she'd be no longer interested in me as a possible victim. I never failed to recognize the speculative gleam in the eye after the first meeting or so. 'Would he be suitable . . . or wouldn't he?' The calculated glance was the first signal to send me on my way. Another warning sign was that she 'took over' the domestics of my boat, insisted on making the tea, that I used the wrong brand of coffee, and once, a very well meaning and domesticated young librarian scooped up a pile of dirty clothes and bedding that had accumulated in a corner of the loo-hole and laundered it all back in her bed-sitter. I'm sure she never understood the reason for my rather sudden disappearance. I had just broken through her virginal reserves and there was all the promise of an interesting and refreshing affair for both of us; but that pile of ironed and folded clothing abruptly terminated my amorous inclinations. She even opened a drawer to put it away 'neatly' as she said. I froze, made the coffee slowly and meticulously, talked eruditely and brightly on canal history and sent her away with a stupid excuse that I was all set to do some work and must do it while the mood was upon me. Dutifully she went and, no doubt, is still mystified why I disappeared so suddenly and so completely. Poor girl . . . .

It has been a glorious spring with hawthorn sprays like lace curtains along the banks of the canal and the surface water filmed over with the blown blossoms; such lavishness and abundance everywhere. The summer followed with long lazy days; endless hours of warmth and light when, to lie on the bank and watch the sun's play through leaves and water, has filled me with an easy content and a sense of completeness and immanence.

Occasionally I phone my sister to keep in touch and to be informed of calamity and celebration. I regretted the last call I made as she ruthlessly demanded that I should take my nephews on board for a week while she went to Scotland to visit an old schoolfriend. Before I could think of a suitable excuse to escape she had given me details of place and time where I should meet them. My sister knows me very well and gave me no opportunity for sliding away from the arrangement. I sighed and said I'd be there; they're really very nice boys – but a whole week; I felt exhausted at the thought of it. I'd have to stock up the larder and get the spare tins of petrol ready as they'd want to be travelling and sight-seeing and generally occupied. It meant getting myself down to Middlewich to meet them, but my sister had given me plenty of time and I could idle my way there without too much effort. The holiday crews were out in force so I chose to do my travelling in the evenings when they were safely tied up and patronizing the local pubs with their noisy talk of marathon achievements and ignorant anecdotes which left the locals in no doubt of their superior knowledge and skills of boat-handling. Also, I like the evenings; the quietness and coolness of the half-light makes no intrusion upon my senses and I can drift down the stretches of canal or river unnoticed and unheard; throttled down my outboard hardly murmurs and the slow wash from the blades barely disturbs the surface.

So, on an evening in mid-June I slid past the moored boats with their lights and television screens and radios and tapes. I tied up for a last coffee, wrote up my diary and thought about a plot for a short story. I didn't feel like sleep and the plot wouldn't come. I felt vaguely restless and decided to go on a little further. A half-moon cast interesting shadows and the stillness of the late evening was in itself an invitation to move on round the next bend. My decision to move was precipitated into action by the ominous sound of an approaching boat and by a beam of light cutting through the shadows. I knew what would happen. Reassurance is needed by all those self-assertive and competent boatmen in peaked caps and to choose a mooring and to tie up seems to throw many of them into a panic of indecision. To see another boat tied up resolves everything.

"Going in here," a voice bellowed. "Get ready with the rope."

I jumped on shore to take a rope, not from any sense of comradeship but because I feared he might well run me down; the sharp stem of his steel boat could so easily slice a hole in my vulnerable fibreglass hull. Luckily, his apprehension had slowed his speed and he came in easily behind me. I tied his fore-end to a branch in the hedge and then started up my own engine.

"I was just moving off anyway," I shouted to the woman still waiting for action on the fore-deck. "Have to make Middlewich to meet a train in the morning."

Lies, but it would salve their self-esteem and I would escape explanations and apologies – all very tedious.

So I escaped and enjoyed moving through shadows and moonlight and the dark wells of uncertainty through the bridge'oles. I half thought of stopping by the Anchorage to renew my acquaintance with it by moonlight. I eased right down so that I was almost drifting along the stretch to the bridge; not the whisper of a breeze in that still night air. *"Plaisir d'amour ne dure qu'un moment,"* I sang away to myself; but this, this would stay with me always.

I thought I could see a gleam of light through the arch of the bridge – maybe it was the moonlight on the water, but I was wary and approached cautiously. I was always wary of possible oncoming boats. I stopped my untuneful singing; surely I could hear music.

"Blast," I thought. "Someone else already there. Shall have to keep going."

I edged the bows neatly through the bridge . . . and then . . .

Automatically I switched off the engine and held the boat steady in the shadow of the bridge.

The place was alive; boats everywhere. I'd have found difficulty in getting through even if I had tried. Nearest to me were the neat sheeted shapes of a loaded pair tied side by side and almost blocking the passage. Behind them more boats, three and four abreast. There were pools of light cast by lanterns on cabin roofs and on the foredecks. All working boats as far as I could see. I took in the scene at an incredulous glance; the open door and unshuttered windows of the pub sent soft shafts of light on to the sloping grassed bank. And the people, they were dressed up for some kind of celebration or event.

"They must be making a film," I thought, and looked around for the cameras; none to be seen or else they were carefully hidden. Perhaps it was a rehearsal for the television programme *The Good Old Days* staged in a natural setting. Whatever it was the set was very convincing.

The music was a dance; then I saw the shadow of a man by the pub door sitting on a chair and playing an accordion. Three couples were engaged in a hopping dance – I supposed it was a polka. I could just make out their costumes, the women in long full skirts and coloured shawls with hair plaited in coils round their heads, and the men in waistcoats over shirts with knotted kerchiefs round their necks; costumes of working people in the twenties I guessed – Sunday or celebration costumes most likely.

It all looked very authentic. My first shocked impression slowly resolved itself into recognition of more specific details. Now I could see that behind the first two boats there was a wide boat with an awning and open sides – a kind of trip boat – and that this was flanked by a single narrow boat, sheeted up and low in the water. Behind these again was a miscellany of loaded and empty boats stretching the length of the frontage and beyond. The whinny of a horse drew my eyes to the hedge at the far end where sheep had made convenient gaps for entry. The gaps seemed to have been patched up and I could see horses, dark shapes standing and cropping. Two more were tethered by the bridge quite near to me and the warm horse smell drifted over on a soft waft of air.

A young lad was prancing about on a kind of hobby-horse and kept charging up to the tied horses in a kind of challenging game. I had a momentary fear that one of them would lash out at the irritation but they stood unheeding and tolerant as he gambolled around them. Funny-looking boy as far as I could see in the light from the already waning half-moon. He wore long short trousers held up by braces, a kind of striped shirt and a man's cap on his head. The boy seemed to be enjoying his part in whatever film it was they were making.

I was about to shout to him when the scene changed to one of purposeful activity. The accordion player stood up and the couples, about six of them, grouped themselves behind him in a kind of procession. Some others and one or two children came out from the pub and joined the group which moved down towards the Cut, the accordion player keeping up a lively tune and the children dancing and anticking around to its infectious melody.

He came to the trip boat and I could see him quite clearly by the light of the lanterns, a dark swarthy man with a large drooping moustache and eyes screwed up as he played. I would have liked to move closer as the view was impeded by the cabins of the other boats, but I was afraid of getting in the way, of cutting across a 'shot' just at the wrong moment. I looked around again for signs of a camera crew and decided that they must be installed in one of the boats below the trip boat. Very quiet though, no shouts or instructions that I would have associated with filming and the players were all remarkably 'natural' and unself-conscious; either they were well rehearsed or this was a trial run to see how the film could be made.

The accordion player now moved back to one side so that I could no longer see him and the couples separated to form an avenue up from the boat. There were giggles and the deeper sounds of men's voices although I couldn't make out any definite words. Perhaps my senses were so concentrated on what I was seeing that auditory perception was dulled. I remember straining to see what those heads, all turned towards the boat, could see already. More lights, lanterns were hooked to the roof of the trip boat by willing hands out of my range of vision. Then a shout from the pub turned my attention away from the boat. In the lit doorway of the pub a single figure had appeared, a man in a tight dark suit; he was young as far as I could distinguish. He came down the grass quite slowly in time to the music which had changed to a sedate marching time. A cheer went up from the couples who now started to clap in time to the rhythm. The lad on the hobby-horse galloped around him, but got in the way and was knocked over by the young man as he moved down through the gap left for him.

"Good old George," shouted a wheezy voice, the first words I had really heard. "Got it coming to him 'e did."

The boy picked himself up and continued his game with the ever-patient horses.

The activity by the boat intensified. I began to identify some of the comments above the general commotion. My boat had drifted slightly and I managed to get a line around the stud on the foredeck of the boat nearest to me. I was still unaccountably reluctant to intrude upon all the activities on the bank.

The voices were raised above the clapping and the music: "Go an' get 'er George . . . She's still waiting . . . Get to it boy . . ." George was hidden in the passage between the couples.

And then I saw her. She stood poised like a spray of hawthorn on the edge of the boat and above the heads of those waiting. I saw her for brief seconds before the arms of the young man reached up and lifted her down and through the ranks of their friends. In that brief instant I caught a glimpse that will never leave me for all eternity. She half-turned as if to look at me and the light from a lantern shone full upon that elfin face, the face of an Ondine, a Dryad, a Nymph, a Nereid – I cannot find the words –

but there she was. Her eyes were dark springs of joy and desolation reaching through the summer darkness to reflect in my own for the barest graze of a second. Then she was gone, lifted down into the arms of her man who had come to claim her. My heart distended with pain as the two of them emerged from the midst of the couples to lead them back into the light of the Anchorage. She was on his further side and I could only catch glimpses of a slender white figure arm in arm with the young man who turned so often to laugh and bend towards her. They were preceded by the accordion player and followed by the other couples, about a dozen or so, all arm in arm. I thought that the small bar would hardly accommodate all of them; perhaps the living-room was also in use for the occasion. As they disappeared the still remembered waves of desolation swept over me, the cold darkness which had first engulfed me in the cellar threatened to prostrate me. I leaned over against the side as nausea threatened. Why? Why? Why? My mind reiterated the only thought of which it seemed capable; and I didn't even know why I asked the question. My wretchedness was broken by a shout from the bank.

The boy with the hobby-horse was prancing along the frontage and must have caught sight of my boat as it drifted out into the channel on the line by which I had attached it, and no doubt he could see me quite plainly standing, or rather leaning, in the well-deck.

"You come to the wedding?" he shouted. "You kin tie up be us – down ther, be'ind *Mabel*," he pointed. "Cum on, I'll ketch yer line."

I felt incapable of action, even of speech. He looked closer and saw the line tying me to the working boat.

"Loose off thee line an' chuck en over," he ordered. "Best get away from they boats quick 'fore George sees 'ee."

Mechanically I loosened the hitch from the deck stud and threw the length of line across to the boy which he caught adroitly, the hobby-horse now abandoned for a more worthy occupation. He flipped the line expertly along the top planks and the cabin roofs of the tied pair and I jerked back into action as my light little boat started to move inwards towards the black side of the hull, stern first, the bows still across the Cut.

"Keep en off will 'ee?" he shouted, "an' tak a turn on t'other

side." No doubt he thought I was a poor kind of boater. No film
star he, an 'extra' no doubt brought over for the take; a younger
member of one of the ex-boaters' families. I was now restored to a
proper frame of mind and concentrated on guiding the *Maybelle*
to a safe gap in the boats and keeping her well away from contact
with the sides of the loaded boats and any others which I might be
passing. The boy seemed to know what he was doing and kept a
wary eye on my manoeuvres as well. Stern first the *Maybelle*
edged past the dark hulls, an empty pair, then the loaded boat
alongside the trip boat, then another pair; ahead were three
abreast and I was just wondering if the line would be long enough
to clear all three when the lad jumped like a cat onto the foredeck
of the outside boat. He took a turn with the line round the stud,
sprang back across the decks of the three boats, then up and over
the cabin tops of the pair picking up a short shaft as he went and
hooking it through the guard-rail of my boat in time to check
it and to stop the bows from swinging outwards; no novice
here.

"I'll tie 'ee up to our back-end," he shouted. "Mam'll not mind.
Thee pull line tight, 'tis tied to Joe's boat; he'll not mind neither,
specially when 'e's 'ad a few . . . Fancy looking boat," he went on
as I followed his instructions and made the line fast to the *Mabel*; I
could just read the name of the outside boat in the light from the
lanterns. *Polly* seemed to be the middle one and I couldn't see the
inside boat. The boy had soon tied up the bows to the stud on the
counter of the motor; no doubt he slept in the cabin if they were
his parents' boats.

"Wot's it made of?" he asked, fingering the side of the hull.

"Fibreglass," I answered briefly.

"Wot glass? Wot's that you said, mister? Our boats is only
wood or the new uns be steel. None about glass though," and he
moved back onto the roof of the inside boat in order to have a
better look. Then he climbed back across the decks of the three to
check my line but really I guessed to have a squint into the cabin
where I had just lit a candle to pour myself a drink.

"It's a special new stuff," I explained. "Doesn't have to be
painted."

"Well, that's something," he said, with a hint of disbelief in his
voice. "My dad would like to know about that. You comin' up
pub fer a drink? They'm all ther. I'm off fer me ale or others'll

drink the lot. Cum on," he shouted as he slipped back across the boats to the bank.

"I'm not asked," I shouted back, coming to my senses. "I must get to Middlewich. Thanks for helping."

Odd sort of boy. Why had I let him tie up? Why had I allowed myself to follow his instructions so that there I was all snug and neatly tied in the only small gap between the boats? I'd have to edge up for'ards to untie the front end and began to do so when the accordion player came out onto the grass followed by the young girl in white and her new young groom.

She must have seen me in the light from a lantern set on the cabin top of the lad's boats. I could see her clearly against the light of the open door and the lad trotted up to her to say something, pointing back in my direction. I was held there in that fix of light from the lantern and the open doorway and I knew that I would not untie the rope which secured the bows to the stern of the motor ahead.

"Come and join us. Come and drink our health. All travellers welcome." The soft slurred voice laughed. "Arrn't they, George?" she asked, waving at me and turning to the young man.

"Aye, that they be. Come ashore and wish us luck," he said. "The luck of a stranger be worth a few drinks. Young Ted 'ere says you've a fancy kind of boat. Come on in an' tell us about it."

I was across the back-ends of the pair to which I was tied and walked their length to take a better look at the trip boat which intrigued me. The bows and the awning were festooned with paper garlands and great clumps of flowers; the heady scent of roses was all about me.

"Come on up then," she called.

The accordion player stopped his tune and leaned elbows on knees to watch me as I crossed the grass, drawn upwards towards the young girl in the pub doorway. There seemed suddenly to be a silence all through that gay, happy gathering and I felt the focus of all eyes as I moved through the silence to the smiling young couple outlined in the lit framework of the door. The dark eyes of the bride held mine despite myself and, as I drew near, a half-startled look flickered between us and a gasp, almost a sigh, broke the silence which seemed to enclose us. She took a step backwards; or was it that her young husband stepped forwards to block the distance between us?

"How do?" he said, his voice already slurred. "Come on in and have a drink. Free on me tonight, for another 'alf hour, any road. Then Rosie an' me'll be off and leave the rest of the drinking to all you lot. Come on, Alec," he shouted across to the still watching musician. "Play up an' get the feet moving. Night's gettin' on. Can't waste time."

The scene came to life again. I was part of that scene, no longer thinking about it as a film, no longer looking for the cameras, no longer aware of time as past, present, future but only as now. I was caught up in the happening there in the old Anchorage pub, no longer an amazed spectator, an outsider, but one whom they all accepted – a traveller whom they welcomed to the wedding of their young friends – relations more like.

The young man threw a brawny arm around his bride and whirled her off round and round down towards the Cut and then back again, followed by other couples, mostly old and middle-aged, but I could also see two or three young couples enjoying the gay jig of the dance in the soft half-light of the cool summer night. The young lad who had invited me was doing somersaults and standing on his head watched by four other younger children who tried to join in his antics. The horses were quietly cropping the turf, unresponsive to the gaiety around them. I found a mug in my hand and a short, red-faced man with a fringe of ginger hair and heavy ginger eyebrows stood by me to watch the dancers.

"Drink up," he said. "Health to the young pair."

"Health to them," I replied mechanically downing the beer – or ale was it? It was cool and tasted of wood and darkness.

"Good beer," I said appreciatively.

"Ale," he corrected, looking me up and down. My jeans and pullover were hardly right for the occasion I realized.

But as I drank and grunted casual comments to the man at my elbow, my eyes and my whole being were drawn and focused upon that light laughing figure being whirled around the grass in the brawny clasp of the young man, her husband. It seemed to me that, although she was caught up in that whirling dance, each time she turned in my direction her eyes were caught in the beam of my own riveted hypnotism. It was as if our eyes were locked into a magnetic field that was generated between us; neither of us could turn away or break from the pull it exerted upon us. In the kaleidoscope of looks caught over the broad back of her husband I read joy and expectancy but also curiosity, fear and despair. Her eyes were wide and dilated with the exertion of the dance and darker with some inner recognition and awareness of what was happening. As for myself, I only felt overpowered and entirely committed, for the first and only time in my life, to the sure knowledge that this lovely elfin girl and I belonged to each other; that, despite her marriage, each of us already knew that a far deeper, more subtle, more fundamental bond between us was being strengthened as each moment passed and by each look trapped with our eyes.

"Young George is a tough customer when crossed," said the man at my side. I turned reluctantly and saw his eyes screwed up in a knowing, half-hostile stare. "Jealous too where his woman's concerned. He'll be off to bed her soon shouldn't wonder. Sooner the better I reckon."

His words hit me heavily as I returned to the reality of the situation. I'd better take my leave while I still had a shred of control left over my moonstruck senses. She wasn't for me, could never be, and the sooner I got away from this strange company whoever they were, the better.

"You wouldn't be the first who's had his eyes on her," he continued. "She's always been a looker. Like a lark her dad always said. But young George 'as been set on her these past three year and at last she agreed to be his mate. New boats they got, too."

"The loaded ones by the bridge?" I asked.

"That's right. Fine new pair loaded at Stoke with ware for Manchester. Good run and a proper start for a pair like George and his Rosie. Taking young Ted with them as his mate so that Rosie don't have to do the heavy work. Allus been spoilt that girl. Where you from?" he added abruptly. "Likely not from round here?"

I was spared the problem of answering as the dance came to an end and the couples returned to the bar for further refreshments. I stood back in the shadows to let them pass.

A short, dark man with another of those heavy 'walrus' moustaches and dressed in a tight, uncomfortable – looking black suit buttoned over a coarse shirt with no tie, sat down heavily on the bench by the wall on the other side of the bar entrance.

"Hey Lil. Cum on out 'ere," he shouted. "Wer's our Rosie?

Cum on gal," he called to her as she and George sauntered up from the new boats they had been looking at. "Not time fer off yet. Another hour an' she'm all your'n son. Not jest yet – a dance with yer ole man, eh Rosie gal?" He waved his beer mug at them and I wondered how he'd stand again to claim his fatherly right.

"Yes Dad, but sober up a bit will you." She laughed and turned to George. "You'll have to hold . . ." She broke off shortly as she caught my eyes where I still stood watching from the shadows by the window shutter. George turned too and I came hastily forwards.

"Hello, I've come to drink your health. Young Ted there," I looked towards the hedge where the lad was feeding one of the horses with tufts of grass. "Young Ted tied up my boat behind the *Mabel* and insisted I come over to drink your health and wish you luck," I ended up rather lamely and suddenly feeling I had no right to be there at all.

"Drink our 'ealth," repeated George heavily and suspiciously. "All travellers welcome to a wedding, specially our'n, hey Rosie?" He pulled her to him as if to indicate his ownership. Her eyes, fearful now, were still upon me and, to break the contact, with some effort I managed to turn away to the bar.

"Another pint, barman," I called through the couples. "Drinks for all on me," I shouted with reckless generosity. I felt in my pocket, a couple of tenpence pieces, how would I pay? I'd have to have a quiet word with the landlord and pay by cheque later on. I tried to catch his eye but he was busy taking orders and filling mugs. Oh well, I'd see him later. Someone passed me a mug of the cool earthy brew and I turned back to George and Rosie. Rosie was over by her dad and the accordion player started up again. The tune was vaguely familiar. Rosie's dad recognized it too and the night air was shaken by a great bass voice that thundered out an unintelligible chorus. All I could make out was, "keep yer 'ands off", followed by a roar of laughing and taken up by the other voices in a ragged attempt to follow the pitch and speed of the accordion player.

"Who *be* you?" asked George under cover of the laughter and the singing. He was really looking at me now, closely, with defiance and curiosity and a slight flicker of fear, or so I thought. "Not one of us be you?"

"Not a boatman, no," I replied. "But I live on the Cut. Do a bit

142

of writing. That's my boat tied up behind the *Mabel* – to Joe's boat I think.''

He looked at me curiously. ''What you on the Cut fer if you ain't got orders? Got some sort of fancy boat young Ted says. Mind if I 'ave a look in the engine 'ole? I like engines. Good steady Bolinder we got – goes like clocks on Sundays.''

''I've only got a small boat,'' I said cautiously.'' You can just make it out from here. Not much bigger than the cabin on one of your boats I guess. Come down and have a look.'' For some reason I was reluctant to take him closer to the *Maybelle*, reluctant to move away from the group of Rosie and her dad, now joined by a stout woman who might just have looked like Rosie many years back and by many others who had drifted out of the bar to join in the song. I was relieved to be gaining the goodwill of George and to see the hostility dissolve into curiosity and interest in another's boat.

It happened that his curiosity was not to be satisfied. The song was over, the tune had changed and the dancing had started again. Rosie was trying to pull her dad to his feet but it was like a moth trying its strength against a crow.

''Come on, Dad,'' she said pulling at him, ''you want a dance, remember?'' But he slumped heavily on the bench and against the wall.

''Let him be,'' said her mother. ''He'll never get further than bed tonight. Go on,'' she said, ''dance with the stranger. Bring you luck. Go on, ask 'im,'' she continued, pushing Rosie towards George and me. Lil was evidently quite 'happy' too. She pushed Rosie right up to me so that I could smell the warm freshness of her. ''Go on, young man, dance with our Rosie and bring 'em both luck.''

It was inevitable. I knew the scene was set for us and we had no choice but to act out our roles.

''All right by you, George?'' but my hand was already on her waist and one light hand rested on my shoulder; a light touch like a brush of hawthorn across the towpath as you walk. There was no waiting for George's reply. We were off on a slow turning dance, watched and then joined by the others. The melody was slow and plaintive and we all turned slowly and soberly to its cadence.

Rosie and I said nothing. We moved as if united in an old ballad

143

which has no beginning and no end but which contains the essence, the inevitability and the immanence of two people coming together as the more blessed, and the more tragic, humans have ever done: Tristan and Isolde, Dante and Beatrice, Romeo and Juliet. The tale is always told, always renewed to tell of the love that transcends time and place, the love that unites and yet is impregnated with the agony of separation.

Her dark eyes, cool and composed now, deeply held mine with an old look of acceptance and certainty. I did not hold her closely; her left hand, gloved in a long scarlet mitten to match the scarlet sash at her waist, rested lightly on my shoulder, so lightly, but I could feel the imprint and pressure through the thickness of my pullover. Her other hand, free of the mitten which she had left with her mother when trying to rouse her father, settled in mine easily and firmly. No need for pressure, our belongingness needed no such superficial gestures.

How long we danced or how we danced I have no idea. I heard nothing but the soft gasp of breath through her lips. I saw nothing but myself in the deep recesses of her eyes as they held mine, and felt nothing but the slow movement of our bodies as they moved in rhythm of the music.

"Kiss the bride. Kiss the bride. All kiss the bride and then she can go."

The words broke in raucously upon the infinitude of our dance and we parted as lightly as we had come together. She was surrounded by the men anxious to claim their lusty rights. "Come on, Rosie gal, give us one back . . . Hope thee'll be a bit hotter fer George later . . . Happen she'm shy . . . Not our Rosie . . . Go on stranger, your turn now," and a shove from behind brought me close to her again. I bent my head and kissed her forehead, how cold it was. She turned her face upwards and kissed my cheek; there never were such virginal kisses exchanged by two such united lovers. But the feel of that kiss is ever with me and the soft pressure of her dear hand in mine is imprinted for all time and wherever I go.

I had some impression of suppressed ferocity as we were parted by the other guests and I turned to be met with a blast of venom and hate.

"I'd slit yer guts if we weren't ready fer off. Watch it next time we meet."

144

I stood there speechless, unable to deny the truth of what the three of us knew. The love of Rosie and myself stood there nakedly and defenceless. George knew it and could only voice his despair and fury through physical violence, the one medium of self-expression with which he was familiar. I fully expected to feel his great fist battering my face – would have welcomed it almost so that in my oblivion I would not be conscious of them leaving together. But a couple of the younger men caught hold of his arms and pulled him towards the waiting boats.

"Don't mess yerself up on account of he," said one. "Your Rosie's waiting fer off. Come on now, here's yer jacket. Good luck . . . still a few hours to mornin'. You jest think o' your Rosie. Lucky bugger. Can't wonder he'd fancy 'er – us all do; but you're the lucky one. Come on now," and slowly they coaxed him down to the boats by the bridge. Someone had started the engine and the steady thump, thump of the Bolinder grew confidently in the late night air.

"Carry 'er on. Carry 'er on. Come on George, do yer stuff. She'm here ready and waiting." The women parted as George shook off his helpers and shrugged a last look of hate in my direction and then moved towards his waiting bride. She stood there, as I had first glimpsed her, a spray of hawthorn with the red breast of a robin settled among the white flowers. He picked her up lightly and set her down in the well on the butty where she stood framed in the light from the open doors of the cabin. The motor-boat edged forward and I crossed onto the bridge for a long last look at her as she slipped away out of sight, out of my life.

The bows of the motor showed through the bridge and I held back out of sight, not wishing to anger George any further by my presence; she would be the one to suffer. The boat checked to pick up the towing line and then moved ahead. He turned once to wave but then resumed his concentration on the route ahead; the dark shadows can be misleading even for an experienced boatman. I could hear the shouts and the cheers and the ribald offers of advice for the hours ahead as the cratch of the butty appeared below me. The shouts and the cheers died as the hull slid through the bridge'ole. The half-moon hung low over the hedge by the towpath and, in its lost light, I saw the cabin top resplendent with jugs of flowers and painted cans and then . . . Rosie.

She stood there, still in her wedding dress, grey now in the fading dark. She was looking upwards as if she knew I'd be there. Our eyes met deeply and with endless longing. The despair and desolation of loss overwhelmed me. If George should kill me I still could not let her drift out of my life. My arms tensed to vault the low parapet of the bridge. She turned her whole self and faced me fully, uplifting her arm as if in eternal farewell. I froze into a temporary death; a real death would have been merciful.

The hand which had rested so lightly on my shoulder was nothing but a bloody, bloody stump, mashed and dripping great gouts of blood onto the deck and the grey whiteness of her dress. She raised it towards me and the sickness of horror gripped my stomach and sent me reeling in revulsion back from the parapet. Horror, love, desolation fractured my senses and I felt nothing but a great coldness and a great emptiness.

I awoke shivering in a grey dawn and with the hard cobbles of the bridge pressed into my back. Without thought, without conscious effort and with heart and senses more dead than in death itself, I crawled back through the broken wicket-gate, which led to the deserted and shuttered pub, across the rough grass filthy with sheep droppings and stumbled into the cabin of the *Maybelle* bobbing lightly on a line tied casually through a ring as if made fast quickly by someone in a hurry to be off. And in my coldness I remembered young Ted and I knew he would have tied up my boat when Joe's boat had moved away from the frontage and then he would have chased up the towpath to join the pair ahead . . . wherever it was they were bound for . . .

There was nothing more in the now familiar handwriting, but in one of the letters an extract from a local paper is included. The extract has been cut out carefully and there is no date, but the copy is faded and yellowed so that it must be old; no doubt an enthusiast for past events could check in the local archives for the original. The extract reads as follows:

LOCAL CANAL TRAGEDY
The Anchorage Claims Another Victim

James Holroyd was discovered two days ago by his young nephews who were to have spent a week's holiday with him on his boat the *Maybelle*. As he was not at the station to meet them they begged a lift from a boat in Middlewich Lock travelling northwards in the hope of meeting up with their uncle's boat. He is well known as an eccentric writer whose absent-mindedness is familiar to them. They saw the boat tied up at the Anchorage, an old bargees' pub which has not been open for several years. Luckily Mr and Mrs Ward who gave the boys a lift waited to see if the uncle was aboard. The boys were shocked and horrified to find their uncle in pools of blood and quite dead. Both his wrists had been cut and foul play is not suspected.

The old pub has the reputation of being haunted and locals will not go there after dark. "A bad place with bad memories," says Ted Smith, an old boatman who now lives in a canal-side cottage in Middlewich. "No one in his senses would tie up there."

"Why do you think Mr Holroyd died like that?" I asked.

"Took on more than he could chew I reckon," said Ted.

According to Ted it seems that one of the old stories about the Anchorage is of a wedding party. The young couple and their relations came there one summer evening for the celebrations. There was a custom that if any other traveller was passing he was called in to kiss the bride and drink the health of the lucky couple. A traveller did call and was invited to wish them luck, but he overstepped the mark and was too familiar with the bride. The usual punch-up for some reason was avoided. The newly-weds set off in their boats, the young man on the motor-boat and his wife on the butty. Instead of stopping the boats just up the canal, which would have been usual as the bride was still in her wedding dress, the furiously jealous husband decided to teach her a lesson. It was dark but he carried on to the next lock. They were using a towing line – often used by experienced boatmen. It passes through the masthead of the butty, through blocks fastened to the top planks and is then secured to a stud on the roof of the butty cabin; the advantage is that the towing line is in the control of the mate on the butty who can shorten or lengthen the line when required. The young woman must have worked it hundreds of times. What happened?

Ted says that she could have made a mistake in the dark, that she had been drinking, that she was terrified of her husband's anger. Whatever it was, as the motor went ahead to pull the butty out of the lock her hand got trapped and caught in the towing line. The figure of eight over the stud tightened as the motor pulled ahead. Either the young man was too far ahead to hear her screams or he thought he'd teach her.

He found her with her hand almost severed covered in blood. "She died from the bleeding," Ted said. "Couldn't get help in time." The young husband was so distraught that he killed himself, cut his throat. They were both found in the butty cabin and rumour has it that they were taken back to the Anchorage and buried in the cellar to save all the enquiries.

Ted says that most of the boat people have heard bits of the story but only half-believed it. It would seem that the tragedy has been repeated with disastrous results for Mr Holroyd and his family.

According to the last paragraph it appears that the reporter had some idea of the story which led to James' death. Or was it mere speculation? After reading the diary and those last tragically written sheets it would seem that he wasn't so far wrong.

The New Bridge

The effort to recreate the story of James Holroyd had occupied reserves of nervous and mental energy for weeks before it had been completed; almost to her satisfaction. Over-concern with thoughts of Hannah's response to her interpretation of the written fragments had often impeded her own imaginative reconstruction. Finally, copies had been sent to Jan and Steph for their appraisal and then further copies to Mary and Hannah. Hannah had written to thank her and to say that Liz could publish it if she so wished. For Liz, Hannah's thanks had been recompense enough. The thought of publishing the growing pile of stories was still too nebulous in her mind to make any serious attempt at a positive effort. Perhaps Noelle would do something with them when she was dead!

Now, without the sprawl of papers to absorb her attention she felt aimless and deflated.

"You're better when you're writing," Noelle said. There had been a stupid row over the cooking; some disagreement about a silly recipe. Both had laughed about it later and Liz apologized.

"My fault; another headache threatening."

"You didn't have a headache all those weeks when you were writing up 'The Anchorage'. Boredom, that's your trouble."

"I can't write all the time – it's too exhausting. Besides I don't have any more ideas. Perhaps I could do some coaching." She didn't sound enthusiastic and both knew that this was no answer to the empty housekeeping days and weeks which now loomed ahead indefinitely.

"You need people," said Noelle. "Although you like to get away by yourself you still need to be with people. You've always been used to having them around."

The next evening she came bursting through the door to where Liz was sitting listlessly in the half-light. She knew that she needed an occupation; too young still just to retire; too active to spend her days just writing. What was there for such as herself? Good works?

"I've got it, Mum." Noelle hardly ever called her 'Mum' and Liz was surprised out of her apathy.

"Local government," said Noelle, cheerfully throwing off her coat. "I've been thinking about it. Some of the oldies need shaking out of their complacency; some of the bright young things need to be kept in order. You're just the person. There's a vacancy . . ."

The months passed; Noelle's prescription had been taken, validated. Liz became immersed in the rounds of committee work yet remained detached enough to enjoy the exchange of opposing opinions and her own carefully chosen contributions to the controversies.

"How d'you do it?" asked Noelle after a skirmish in a housing committee attended by both mother and daughter.

"A lot of homework. No one can argue against the facts, although facts can be elusive. The evidence has to be sifted, has to be cast-iron," Liz had replied. "That's what I enjoy – coming in with the evidence after all the opinionated hot air; power I suppose. But you have to win where people are concerned. So, I have to get the logistics right – as they say – before I go into the committee room."

"Know what you mean," said Noelle. "Takes time though. Worth it to see their faces," and they had both laughed at the recollection of complacent pomposity deflated by Liz's carefully prepared 'logistics' delivered like clear rain on the pool of their pretentious solecisms.

"Good idea to straighten out that bad bend while we're about it," said Ken Smallwood at the local council meeting. He was a short, energetic man, dressed almost always in a duffel coat and the better kind of green wellington boots with straps to tighten when the rain was heavy; thick, white woollen socks folded over the tops made the neat transition between boots and cord trousers. He sat with hands thrust deep into sagging pockets, his hard brown eyes noting and registering every detail of response to his suggestions about the new bridge on the face of the councillors around the table. They were a conservative lot, slow to commit themselves to the firm decision which would authorize the go-ahead for Smallwood's project. He knew that this meeting was crucial; it could continue for hours; further discussion could be delayed for days on various pretexts despite the lengthy reports, proposals, costings and estimates for the work which had been sent to every member three months before and which now lay imposingly in the neatly bound buff coloured folders on the table before each of the councillors. Many were still unopened and retained the look of pristine non-usage while others were well-thumbed and even annotated with pencilled comments. Smallwood noted these with a wry inward smile; he knew what he was up against and knew that he would need to curb his own impatient demand for action. He was young – too young some had said at his recent appointment – and he was aware that his job as consultant surveyor to the newly formed County Council would require resources of tact and diplomacy as well as confidence in his own ability and expertise. There were still factions between the old councillors of the Borough and those of the Rural

Council and a resentment of both towards the newer 'upstarts' who represented the influx of overspill population from London. Smallwood noted that, on the whole, the folders of the last contingent were those which had been most thoroughly examined. He'd have their support and, if he was careful, the support of the old Borough councillors. He knew from the set of their mouths and the way they talked among themselves, ignoring him, that the representatives of the rural district were against him and his project. It would be a tedious business before he could get going and the precious weeks of summer and fine weather could be lost.

Smallwood's interest in canals was cursory and incidental to his work. He was friendly with Charles, the owner of a local boat-hiring firm to whom he had given unofficial advice on the building of a new marina. They had met at a local Rotarians' dinner; Smallwood had thought it prudent to align himself with the right institutions of the town. They met subsequently at the comfortable pub adjacent to the new marina. He had hired a boat for a couple of weeks and, with a compliant girl-friend from Weybridge where he had worked previously, had 'done' one of the regular trips as advised by Charles. The relationship with the girl was a casual affair and not improved by the two weeks of close proximity.

It had rained for the greater part of the second week and, apart from his interest in bridge construction, the variety of canal-side buildings and the new estates through which the canal winds, Smallwood found the trip tedious. The slow speed irked him; Annette's cooking was indifferent and her sexual responses inhibited. He could have covered the distance by car in a couple of hours and enjoyed a more expansive holiday in Corfu. Charles had persuaded him that he should know the canals in the area and that the only way to survey bridges and tunnels was from the cockpit of a boat and if he knew a girl . . . well, what better place than a boat for a holiday affair. He had phoned Annette half hoping she couldn't or wouldn't come; she had tried not to sound too eager. The two weeks passed slowly, although Smallwood reluctantly enjoyed his growing efficiency in handling the boat and being moored neared Campden Lock gave them both a few days' respite from each other's company. Smallwood had gone off to visit his brother and family while Annette stayed to look after the boat. He was away for an extra day and the return trip back to the marina was something of a scramble against time – the boat was booked for the following week. It was late, he was tired, and he crashed the boat into the bank round the bad bend just before reaching base. On the outward journey Charles had been with him to explain the controls and had warned him to throttle right down when approaching the bend. He'd forgotten and was annoyed with himself for forgetting. What a stupid way to travel anyway. The brambles tore at the paintwork and he'd have to explain the scratches. Annette shoved away uncomplainingly with the long shaft from the roof top and they were free without too much effort. The thirty-foot boat had a shallow draught and the heavy rain had raised the water level. Charles had laughed when Smallwood apologized for the scratches.

"You aren't the first; almost everyone crashes the bridge or the bank – usually both. We're well covered by insurance and a few licks of paint works wonders. I bet the North brothers had a grin to each other when they heard the crash."

"They live in the cottage by the bridge? Who did you say?"

"The North brothers, Jack and Bert. Worked on the Cut at one time but have been retired for years, long before I came here. There used to be a sister too, but she's dead long ago. Queer old boys – never talk to anyone and live behind their dingy lace curtains."

Smallwood wasn't interested.

"That bend now," he said. "It's ridiculous – the bridge too. What a stupid place to have built one." An idea began to germinate.

"That bridge must take some hammering," he continued later over lager and sandwiches at the Globe. "I see quite a lot of heavy stuff taking this side road."

"Not supposed to," said Charles. "A couple of lorry drivers live in the village – take their lorries through to spend the night at home. It's a quick way through the lanes to the town; saves the pile-ups at the roundabout and the traffic lights. Quite a few seem to be using the back way these days."

"You must have a fair bit of traffic to your place in the summer."

"Quite a bit."

"And that bridge isn't going to stand up to that kind of use

much longer. Right? A skewed bridge too; dangerous to lorries as
well as boats."

"I know what you're thinking," Charles had said with a laugh
"A nice straight bridge, a nice straight canal and lots of prestige
for you with the new council."

"Could be." Smallwood was a cautious man until he had fully
assessed a new proposition, but once he had become familiarized
with the possibility of achievement he became a man of action.

His memory scanned some of the preliminary events as the
Chairman droned on about the project – *his* project.

"You'll be up against some of the locals and the canal enthusiasts," Charles had warned him, but Smallwood didn't take that
too seriously. A wide new bridge like the one further up the canal
over the A5 would provide a good major route into the town from
the motorway and relieve much of the congestion on the present
exit road. Localized transport would be better served and Smallwood reckoned that any scheme which provided an easier system
to and from the town to the motorway would gain enough
support to outweigh localized objections based on such irrelevan-
cies as 'historic and aesthetic values', 'interests of the rambling
society' and other such trivia from the rather emotional and
esoteric groups of enthusiasts who resented change in the ever-
changing landscape around them.

The Chairman had finished at last, and a young woman was
standing. She held a folder of her own, adjusted a pair of heavy
spectacles and began to read from a prepared paper.

"There's a humanitarian aspect to this proposed siting of the
new bridge," she began, then looked directly at Smallwood who
felt just the slightest twinge of apprehension at the directness of
her look through those overlarge spectacles.

"Too heavy for her face," he thought irrelevantly.

"Is it not true," she asked after a suitable pause to fix his
attention, "that the cottage by the bridge will have to be demolished if the new bridge is to be built on the site that is
proposed?"

"Of course," he replied shortly. "The plans and surveys for the
bridge are in the folder." The implication was taken.

"I have studied the plans and read your proposals in some
detail," she replied calmly without removing her eyes from his
face. He began to resent this officious young woman; one of the

'upstarts' no doubt. (Whose side were they on?)

"The cottage is inhabited by two old men, two very old men," she continued. "They have been associated with the canal all their lives. To lose their home could destroy them. What does the County Surveyor propose to do about them?"

He was ready for this. He picked up his pencil, studied it and proceeded in a level, reasonable voice. "There are cases in the paper every day similar to this; people who refuse to leave their houses when the rest of the community is making demands for new roads, new factories, new housing estates . . . even new bridges. They all get rehoused and it's surprising how many of them actually enjoy the comforts of a new flat or bungalow once they are moved – and all at the council's expense. It's the actual decision they find so hard to make. If it's made for them there's a protest; we leave time [Christ, we have so little time; all this fine weather] to let them get used to the idea, a little financial persuasion and they settle again surprisingly easily. If you read up the protest cases you will find that almost all of them follow the same pattern."

"Where do you propose to rehouse the North brothers? The canal is part of their lives. Have you a property in mind adjacent to the canal where they could live out their days?" she questioned with a calm, detached voice. "If only she'd get a bit excited," Smallwood thought, "most females do; but this one, she's like . . ." He couldn't think; she was still fixing him to give her his attention. Several heads were beginning to nod approval and many faces were looking at her expectantly and sympathetically. He must swing the meeting to support him and his proposals. Two old men. Calmly he opened his own folder and extracted a sheet of paper. "Skew Bridge Cottage," he read. "No supply of water except from a shallow bore in the garden which dries up during the summer. No sanitation, a privy at the end of the garden. Evidence of rat infestation along the canal frontage. Madam, Mr Chairman, Councillors, it would seem to me a real service to these two elderly gentlemen to rehouse them in more comfortable and sanitary conditions for their declining years. There is a ground floor flat available in the new complex recently built for senior citizens in Alexandra Square. I have personally seen the Housing Officer and there will be no problem in reserving the flat for them."

The faces swung around in his direction and the nods of approval reassured him of the change in his favour.

"But," she continued to speak. Why didn't the Chairman give the nod to the bald young man down at the far end who was lifting two fingers like a Scout signal each time there was a pause in the proceedings? She continued relentlessly, calmly, voice still firm and on the same level.

"Officious little madam," thought Smallwood. "Woman enjoying her moment of power." He had no time for women in public affairs.

"Is it possible to imagine Jack North and his brother living in the centre of town?" she asked the meeting. It was, indeed, difficult to imagine. Most of those present knew the brothers at least by sight. For years after the working boats on the canal had almost ceased to operate they had worked a coal round in the surrounding villages and their faces and hands were so ingrained and pitted with the stuff that it was doubtful it could ever be removed, even with daily baths – supposing they could be induced to remove their coal-impregnated overcoats which they wore indoors as well as out. To imagine them living within the scrubbed and painted sterility of the new complex – of which the Councillors were inordinately proud – registered alarm and apprehension. It wouldn't do at all and again the faces turned hopefully to the young woman.

"It wouldn't do at all," she confirmed their doubts. "Perhaps Mr Smallwood does not know that the Norths and their sister were rehoused only ten years ago so that their previous cottage could be demolished to make way for the new bridge over the A5. Their sister was blind and she took the loss of the cottage, in which she had lived, very badly. Luckily for them this present cottage was empty. The Waterways Board, to whom it belongs, was willing for the North family to rent it when they had to leave their own. But the blind sister never really settled and used to tap her way back to the ruins of the home where she had lived for so long."

A voice from a seat below the centre of the table where Smallwood sat interrupted the young woman. "I remember her, Blind Polly she was called. I used to see her when I went there fishing as a boy. She used to sit outside the cottage with her knitting and hail the boats as they went by. 'Seen my brothers?'

she'd call out and, 'What boats be you?' All the boat people knew her.''

"Did she die then?" asked Smallwood, caught up in the interest of the group.

"She was killed, Mr Smallwood," said the level voice, almost accusingly. "She went out every day as her cottage was destroyed – you can still see the foundations on the bank below the bridge – and then, one day she was knocked down and killed by one of the lorries which came thundering past on the straight new stretch of wide road over the bridge. No one knew exactly what happened. She's buried in the churchyard where she walked to church three miles there and back each Sunday."

"That's right. I've heard people from the village say that you could tell the time on Sundays by the tapping of Polly's stick."

Ken Smallwood shrugged himself out of a passing interest; the old girl was dead and her two brothers still alive in their old ruin. "More's the pity," he thought.

"Well," he said brusquely in the following pause having caught the Chairman's eye. "The past is the past and the new bridge in the Heyford lane is as necessary now as the bridge over the A5 was necessary ten years ago. Can't hold up progress." He hated the stupid cliché, but so often it was acceptable as a definitive statement to justify a decision and he thought it the right phrase for the situation.

He underrated his councillors. The man with the Boy Scout gesture succeeded in his effort to be heard. The young woman had seated herself, almost opposite to Smallwood, and carefully replaced her papers.

"There's a point, you know, we all seem to have forgotten," said the bald young man earnestly. "These two brothers are getting on a bit. How old did you say they were, Miss?" He looked for help to the young woman. Now that he was on his feet his nervousness became apparent and he looked hopefully for support.

"First-timer," thought Smallwood. "No threat." Again he was wrong.

"Eighty-nine and ninety-one respectively," she replied.

"Well then, they won't live forever," said the man facetiously. "Why not compromise and delay the project for a year or two? The old men might well be ill . . . or worse . . . in that time; then we have no problem. Besides there's the expense." He sat down abruptly. Murmurs of agreement and support were ominous.

But Smallwood held the trump card. He wanted this project to go ahead very badly. It was his first big job with the Council; he enjoyed building bridges and he saw this as an opportunity to prove himself, to establish himself with this Authority. Whatever he thought of them as persons they represented the power and authority which paid his salary – and such jobs were becoming increasingly hard to come by – and gave him scope for realizing some of his ambitions.

"It's a good idea." He smiled agreeably at the woman who did not respond. "And I had already decided that this would be the right approach. The old men, as you rightly suggest, are unlikely to survive for many more years. In fact, I heard locally that one has been very ill with 'flu and is still extremely weak. I did think that healthwise they would be better off in a flat with central heating; but Mr Able may well be right." He paused, then withdrew another sheet from the bulky folder before him. "Unfortunately, the building cannot be delayed indefinitely. I have made a thorough survey of the structure and on the underneath of the bridge a fairly wide crack is apparent. Over the past three months the crack has extended by twelve centimetres and the width at base extended to two centimetres; a serious situation as many of you will appreciate. In my estimation the bridge will not last another six months, taking into consideration the weight of summer traffic which I understand is extremely heavy and increasing all the time. The new marina will attract a good many visitors and the heavy plant for servicing the boats, supplying provisions and equipment will make more extensive use of the side road on which the site has its main access. Another few months of heavy traffic and I wouldn't like to be answerable for what could happen."

There was silence; uncertainty and doubt registered round the table. The Chairman coughed. "How long would it take to build a new bridge?" he asked.

"The best estimate I have here in terms of time is for three months from the date of order." Smallwood had his facts and figures ready. He mentioned a well known local firm of contractors; a bit pricey but a good reputation. "They're ready to give the job top priority," he continued, anticipating the usual question.

"That would mean the job would be finished by June; not quite in time for the early part of the season but better than having to close the road throughout the summer."

"Bad as that?" the Chairman enquired, and Smallwood nodded. "Right, ladies and gentlemen, we have to make a decision." The Chairman was on his feet prepared to give a lengthy summing up of all the relevant facts in order to get a decision from the councillors. It was imperative to reach a decision, and in his mind he was certain what that decision should be; he backed Smallwood. The urgency of the safety factor was uppermost; he too was not anxious for any adverse publicity on the subject of safety. The Press could be very virulent about priorities, about imprudent economies and the recent expenditure on the new shopping precincts. This was his first term of office as Chairman of the Council and he too saw the project in terms of his own reputation. Smallwood leaned back with a half-smile of satisfaction as he listened; the new bridge would be built.

"There seems to be no reasonable doubt about the necessity for a new road bridge to replace the old one," the Chairman concluded. "The only problem remains is where to rehouse the North brothers, but, if we are agreed to sanction the proposal, then it seems that the cottage will have to go."

The murmurs of assent and agreement were sharply interrupted by a hard rapping. Smallwood jerked to attention; the rapping had seemed to come from the table directly in front of him and he had a momentary flash-back of having his knuckles rapped with a ruler by an irascible schoolmaster. Instinctively he thrust his hands down into the pockets of his duffel coat, looked up to meet the eyes of the young woman opposite; she looked amused. The Chairman called out "Come", and the door opened to admit a secretary who apologized for interrupting and she handed him a note. Smallwood slumped back again in his chair; he could have sworn that the rapping had been on the table in front of him but obviously he was mistaken; tired, tensed, he needed a drink. The young woman had removed her glasses; she watched him quizzically. He glared back and relapsed into passivity, looked at his watch, almost one o'clock; the others would be thirsty too.

"Urgent business," said the Chairman. "Ten minutes and you'll have to excuse me."

The meeting rushed to a decision. The balding Scoutman had made notes and importantly rose to formulate the proposition that a new bridge be constructed and that the local firm should immediately be invited to submit full details of costs and design.

"The one problem of the Norths' cottage remains," he said hesitantly. "I propose that Miss Christie undertakes to make contacts with the Health Department and the Housing with the intent of getting them rehoused – in their own interests," he added hopefully.

"We have two proposals," said the Chairman. "One at a time. We must ask Miss Christie if she consents to accept the responsibility for the brothers."

Miss Christie knew that she had no choice. As the Health Visitor such problems were usually referred to her accompanied by the usual facetious gallantries from the men who did the offloading. She listened to the words – "In your capable hands . . . with sympathetic tact . . ." She cut short the banalities. "I'll do what I can," she said coldly.

Smallwood felt a small pang of sympathy for the woman – Miss Christie was she? He was glad to be a builder of bridges; people now were different.

The Councillors voted and unanimously passed both resolutions. As the meeting broke up into garrulous groups he followed the Chairman out through the door and found that she too had escaped. Momentarily they were alone in the small vestibule which led out into the main hall.

"Sorry to have landed you with such a problem," Smallwood said moving out of that narrow confine. She had let him precede her and he turned to catch a reply. She stood in the half-light, those ridiculous spectacles looking grotesque on the small face.

"You may well be sorry," she replied. "Maybe you have taken on more than you realize."

"Now, just what do you mean by that?" asked Smallwood, turning abruptly and making for the outer door. "Come and have a drink," he added impulsively.

"No thanks," she replied. "I have a case waiting for me," and she turned down one of the corridors leading off from the hall.

"Hell," said Smallwood to himself, wishing he hadn't offered.

He was caught up immediately in the business of getting the

project started. A whole week went by seeing the contractor, getting estimates finalized and submitted, and contacting the various authorities who would in some way be affected by the building. At the end of the week he met Charles for the usual pub lunch.

"Cheers," said Charles affably. "To success and a new bridge."

"Worse to come," replied Ken Smallwood. "It's not going to be such an easy job. That angle . . . really needs the canal to be straightened out first. That ridiculous bend."

"Not a hope," returned Charles. "Major operation that . . . and no money."

"I know, I know. I'll have to do the best I can," said Ken irritably.

"By the way," continued Charles, "anything been done about the North brothers? I hear that Polly's up and around again."

"Polly? Polly who?" Smallwood's mind was cluttered with lists and prices and interviews and technicalities.

"Blind Polly. You must have heard of her. Sister of the North brothers. I guess she objects to the cottage being knocked down."

"What *are* you talking about? She's dead, isn't she?"

"Dead, but won't lie down," guffawed the bearded Charles. "Kitty in the shop says that Polly won't let you get away with it."

"Whatever nonsense are you talking about, Charles? Come on. I've got work to do."

Charles looked at him, an odd look thought Ken as he caught the other's eye.

"Not such nonsense, Ken," he said seriously. "I heard Polly myself when I came here first. I used to hear her tapping away along the road at the top – up and down. It rattled me until I grew almost used to it. Haven't heard it now for a couple of years. She decided I was harmless I guess and let me stay."

"Never heard such rubbish. You of all people, Charles, to be superstitious."

"I'm telling you what I heard," replied Charles. "There was no other explanation I could find for that tapping along the road. I used to go and watch . . . but there was nothing, just the tapping that went off down the road and gradually stopped. When she's angry, though, the tapping changes to a hard rapping sound – like this," and he rapped with his knuckles on the table. Ken heard again the rap on the table during the Council meeting.

161

"Doing a Polly?" laughed the barman.

"Trying to tell my friend here that she's still around. He doesn't believe me."

"If he's going to build that bridge he'll soon find out."

Smallwood looked at his watch. "I'll keep an open mind. Must be off," he said, feeling more cheerful after his couple of pints.

He drove down the road, towards the village. A cheerful red car, a DAF he noted, was parked outside the Norths' cottage. The young woman, Miss Christie, was just getting out as he approached and, on an impulse, he drew up behind and also got out. She looked surprised and waited for him to speak.

"I'll come in with you, shall I?" he asked. "I feel a bit responsible although you may not think so."

"You are entirely responsible, but then you think in terms of construction and destruction whereas I think in terms of people." She rummaged in the back of the car; Smallwood stood his ground, not to be dismissed so easily. She had nice legs.

She emerged with a bottle of medicine and a small package. "I suppose you might as well come in and meet the objects of our differences now that you're here." She tried always to be rational, necessary if you worked with men whose irrational contradictions always accused the female of being emotional instead of logical. "You won't be asked in," she said tapping on the door; no bell, no knocker and the door half-grown over with ivy and untended rose briers. No answer, but Smallwood saw the edge of a lace curtain lifted and heard the deep growl of a dog.

"Someone there, the curtain's pulled back," he said.

"They pretend to be deaf," said Miss Christie as she knocked again – harder. "They're probably suspicious of you too."

Smallwood walked past the window and into the yard still littered with left-overs from the coal round: an old cart, some heavy scales of an old design, odd piles of different sized coal, and black dust everywhere. Even the branches of an apple tree which overhung the yard were blackened with the stuff. A large rat broke cover from one of the piles and disappeared round the back of the cottage where Smallwood could see the line of the canal. He wanted to take a better look at the bend from the back of the cottage but, as he turned through the gap in the old fence round the yard, Miss Christie called to him.

"Someone's coming."

He turned; no need to antagonize the old boys by taking liberties on their property.

The door opened fractionally.

"It's only me," she said. "I've come to see how your brother is today and brought him a pick-me-up from the doctor. Can I come in?"

The door opened wide enough to let her in. Smallwood hesitated outside, still no one to be seen in the dark doorway.

"I've brought along someone who'd like to talk to you about the old days on the canal," her voice continued.

Smallwood regretted his impulse; it would do no good to see the old boys and Miss Christie sounded capable enough to deal with them.

"You'd better come in," she called as the door remained open.

"I think I'd . . ." he began.

"Come on in – quickly," she cut him short sensing his reluctance.

He pushed in through the door, curious despite himself. The gloom of the room darkened by curtained windows was relieved by a cheerful fire in the grate at the far end. A small hunched figure in cap and greatcoat sat huddled in a large straight-backed chair pulled close on to the hearth. A large shaggy collie which lay stretched in front of the fire looked up suspiciously, a low growl in its throat. The old man in the chair put out a hand to touch its back and the animal slunk away under his chair.

"How are you today, Mr North?" asked the young woman putting the medicine and package on the table.

"He's just middling, Miss. Don't eat much," said the one who had opened the door.

"Mr Smallwood," she said lifting a hand to indicate him. "Mr Bert North."

"Sorry about your brother. Hope he's soon well again." Smallwood looked at the old man by his elbow, old black overcoat tied round with a good leather belt, grey bristly chin, sharp little foxy eyes under the peak of a cap blackened with grease and coal.

"What you want to know?" he asked suspiciously; then, "Polly's up again." It sounded like a warning and an accusation. Miss Christie was occupied with the old humped figure in the chair; no support from her.

"Polly? Your sister?" he asked.

163

"Always about if there's mischief," said Bert, keeping his sharp eyes on Smallwood. Smallwood stood there by the table covered with a faded green chenille cover; a half-cut loaf, pot of jam, teapot – dust everywhere he noted; no chair except the two by the fire; a glimpse of the canal through the lace curtains at the back, the sound of a boat's engine.

"You live on the Cut?" asked Bert. Without waiting for an answer he continued: "We used to work the boats, Jack and me. Coal down from Griff – closed now. Mam worked the business from this end."

It was a liturgy he had often repeated for the casually curious summer visitors and there was no interest or inflexion in his voice.

"Hard life it was." In the pub this usually meant a free pint or two from crews of the smart 'noddies' greedy for some real local colour from the past. "Such a character . . . you never saw such clothes . . . never had a bath in his life . . . amusing old boy . . . the real McCoy . . ." Bert was cynic enough to give them what they wanted as he noted the women edge away and the men guffaw immoderately over the more basic details of life on the boats. He was an artist and embroidered his memories to suit the audience. His brother Jack was a recluse and a teetotaller. "Like Mam," Bert used to say in his defence, "I was the wild one."

His eyes were sizing up Smallwood's response. A hard one. Smallwood ignored the information and moved to the window to watch a passing boat.

"So Polly's round again." Miss Christie had given Jack some of the medicine, put the bottle again on the table.

"Heard about the bridge I reckon," said Bert. Smallwood turned sharply; so the old boys knew. "She don't think much on it." Smallwood felt accused once more, then angry at feeling anything. This was business.

"The bridge is dangerous and will have to be rebuilt," he said briefly.

"Like Globe bridge." Bert spoke sharply.

"A good straight bridge to take the traffic." Smallwood wanted to get away from the dingy room and the ferrety little man. The humped figure by the fire drew more closely into the chair; the dog continued to growl softly, intermittently.

"Polly don't like it," Bert repeated.

"Polly doesn't live here. She's dead isn't she?" Smallwood sounded brusque, impersonal. "You and your brother will be given a new flat in town, well heated – a doctor for your brother, shops . . . everything."

"What about t'Cut?" the wheezed voice came from the chair.

Then Smallwood heard it – rap – rap – rap, in the room over their heads.

Miss Christie looked up. "Polly," she said.

The tapping moved up and down the room, slowly at first and then with increased vigour.

"Someone's up there; it's some joke," said Smallwood coldly.

"It's Poll's room," said Bert; he spoke as if she were indeed still up there.

"You won't find anyone," said Miss Christie, "but she's there all the same."

"You get out," Bert's voice was sharp. "You get out. She don't like you. And we don't leave the Cut. Jack and me, we live here."

Smallwood was glad to be out in the fresh spring air as the door was closed and bolted behind him. Miss Christie had chosen to come as well. They walked to the gate in silence; the tapping seemed to follow them but at a distance. Miss Christie made no comment.

"What's behind all this Polly business?" asked Smallwood as she opened the car door.

"I think you know," she replied heavily. "Polly may be dead . . . but . . ."

"I know – more things in earth and heaven."

"I can only tell you that her tapping indicates anger, annoyance, anxiety with some event which affects her brothers and their connection with the Cut, as they call it. You heard what Bert said – she doesn't like the idea of the new bridge and is angry at the proposed loss of their cottage."

"Well, whatever the cause a bit of tapping isn't going to stop me. If that's all it won't bother me. You go ahead, Miss, with rehousing those old boys – they could also do with delousing."

"You don't care, do you?" Smallwood noted with satisfaction the spark of anger in her voice. "They're just bundles of rags to be disposed of. Did you know that their nephew is quite a well-known solicitor? Lives in London and comes over to keep an eye on them. They're worth quite a bit so all the locals say . . .

Perhaps you should take Polly's warnings more seriously."

She got into the car.

"But look here," Smallwood wanted her support not her antagonism, "what would you do? That bridge is dangerous. I'm not inventing the crack. Come and have a look, or ask Charles if you don't believe me."

"I believe you all right; you could hardly invent such a reason for rebuilding. But couldn't you site the bridge elsewhere – down nearer the village?"

"And rebuild stretches of road? There's the road from Flore."

"Almost unused and could be closed." Obviously she had been thinking of a solution. It would 'up' the costs as the road would have to be entirely re-routed. The Council wouldn't stand for it, he reasoned; there was no other way.

"Couldn't it be patched, reinforced or whatever you can do to old bridges?" She started the engine. "The solicitor could be difficult. He's fond of the old boys."

Smallwood shrugged and moved back as she let in the clutch. The raps didn't disturb him. The solicitor might prove to be a more tangible opponent. He'd have to check again on the legalities of eviction.

"Might as well have another look," he thought, walking down the road and onto the towpath. The tapping followed; he turned once or twice – no one, and when he turned the tapping ceased. It nettled him despite his pragmatic attitude to all events, natural or otherwise. He knew about psychic phenomena of course, and accepted the fact that it was experienced, but had never met up with anything himself; he was not interested, he worked with facts and estimates. Polly might indeed be resentful on behalf of her brothers but there was nothing she could do about it. She was dead and he had a bridge to build. However, there was nothing to lose by having another look. From the shelter of the bridge he surveyed the cottage on the opposite bank; it was so obviously the right, the only place to span the canal; a nice straight after the bend and the village road would need only three hundred yards of re-routing; or possibly it could be closed. The suggestion of closure had been proposed but was squashed by an influential local farmer who had claimed his rights of access. What about the other side of the bridge? Smallwood had considered this alternative many times but the ground on both sides of the canal was

marshy and low-lying and the canal itself widened and wound again so that in no way was the building of a bridge there feasible. He stood under the arch of the bridge; could the old structure be reinforced? It was so steeply humped and so skewed that he dismissed the solution as impracticable as he had done so often during the previous weeks. No, he decided, his decision to build a new bridge where the old cottage stood had been the right one; it was the only possible and strategically suitable place to put the bridge. Suddenly a sharp and vigorous prod in the back sent him staggering and before he could regain his balance he was in the Cut. It wasn't deep and his feet soon found the muddy bottom; getting out wasn't so easy. Christ, what a fool he felt; no one in sight for the moment; the water was icy and his feet were sinking into the mud. He put his hands onto the coping to heave himself out; the rapping had started again, quite near at hand, and again there was a smart cut across the back of his hand which made him momentarily draw back. "Sod you, Polly," he shouted. "Clear off will you," and he pulled himself out of the water back onto the towpath, one boot and sock sucked off by the mud. He sat with his back against the wall of the bridge to recover; took off his duffel coat to shake and pulled off the other boot to empty out the water. The blue flash of a kingfisher caught his eye as it flew almost level with the water to perch on an overhanging branch from the old apple tree in the coal yard. As his eyes followed it he saw the lace curtain in the back room of the cottage twitch and knew he was being watched. "Sod the old boys, sod Polly, sod the canal, sod the bridge, sod everything," he muttered as he replaced the boot on one foot and put the sodden sock on the other, squeezed out his trouser legs as well as was possible, draped the coat round his shoulders and edged his way up the muddy path at the side of the bridge to the road. He wasn't taking any more chances with Polly around. How Charles would laugh if he knew. He looked back at the water; a ditch, just a bloody ditch; what a stupidity to cause such problems. He limped back to the car; luckily no one seemed to be around although the rapping was loud enough to be heard even with the car windows closed. He turned on the engine, moved the car off down the road to get away from Polly and her stick, turned on the heater to warm up his frozen feet – he had removed his other boot – and didn't stop until he was on the far side of the village where he pulled up only long enough to fetch an old pair of plimsolls from the boot to make driving less of a hazard and rather more comfortable than with his bare feet. After such ignominious treatment by Polly and her damned stick he was even more resolved to build the bridge and build it in the most obviously suitable place; Polly and her brothers would have to take up residence elsewhere.

It was the end of June before the work was finally started and the first signs of activity became apparent to the local residents. A site hut was erected with wires from the nearby electricity and telephone cables connected and a JCB gouged out a lay-by for itself in the bank on the far side of the bridge from the cottage. Piles of steel rods and heaps of concrete blocks were dumped on the roadside verge. Children of all ages appeared to gawp and warily to test their climbing and balancing skills on the inviting piles.

"Keep those kids away," shouted the foreman, and a police panda car was enlisted to patrol twice a day to warn off the would-be vandals.

Smallwood was kept busy eighteen hours a day with petty irritations and hindrances; he found it difficult to delegate. He was lucky with the foreman, a cheerful, competent Irishman employed by the firm for the past twenty years. He had a rough tongue and used it, but seldom lost a man on the job; he was known by all as 'Paddy'. Smallwood forgot about re-checking the legalities of eviction, or rather he had put off the business in the welter of more immediate and pressing problems to be dealt with.

"Once the work is under way," he thought as the machines began to be assembled and the date for demolition drew near, "I'll just check. No need really, BWB gave permission, agreed compensation; can't be any other angle."

He hadn't seen Miss Christie since the day they had visited the brothers, since he had slipped into the Cut – as time passed the notion that he had been pushed seemed more and more improbable, he was letting himself become rattled with all those tales, with his own barely acknowledged feeling of guilt about the old boys and their precious home – and there had been no sign of life from the cottage except for the thin spiral of smoke from the end chimney. The site office had been erected at the end of the cottage 'garden' where the old wall had crumbled so that the 'garden' merged into the overgrown bank bordering the canal. The hut was furnished sparsely with a table, filing cabinet, a bed and a gas cooking-stove. A watch would be needed through the nights to keep an eye on materials and machinery. An air-gun was put in an obvious position and a shot or two at the angry rooks served as a warning to would-be pilferers. Paddy lived in lodgings and had no apparent family, although it was hard to imagine such a flamboyant and colourful character without wife, children and a trail of 'acquaintances'. Whatever his history, at the time he declared he had no ties and opted to use the site hut as his temporary home.

"Like to keep me eye on things," he said to Smallwood, "and gives me a bit o' spare fer the bar – not on the job o' course," he added as Smallwood hesitated. "Handy with me fists, the gun too if I have to be." Well over six feet and with shoulders which stretched the already split leather jacket, he would soon put the fear into local yobs. So it was agreed; while the job was on Paddy would live in the 'office'.

"I like a place to meself," he added when Smallwood mentioned the lack of comfort, "and there's the bar just up the road if I get lonesome."

"What about the old boys?" he asked a couple of days later. "What happens when th'ould cottage comes down?"

"They're going to be rehoused, a new flat in town; a week's time I think." Smallwood hadn't heard anything definite himself; he'd have to check. No immediate hurry as there were pilings to be sunk on the opposite side to the cottage. Better to move them soon though.

"Powerful lot of rats," said Paddy. "Have to put down the poison."

"Careful where you put it. The brothers have a dog. Don't want more problems."

"Have to get rid o' the animal whatever; no pets in Council flats. Plenty of talk about it in the bar," he confided. "The locals don't like you much. They say old Poll's on the warpath; been heard all over the place. Don't scare me though."

"What should you be scared of?" asked Smallwood.

"Well," said the Irishman slowly, "she come knocking on my door last night. Moonlight it was, clear as day, there weren't no one there – but this rapping on the door . . . stopped me sleep for a couple of hours."

Smallwood shrugged; this blind Polly should be exorcized. No time . . . and he was sceptical of the mumbo-jumbo.

"Can't hurt you, a lot of rapping . . . lots have heard it. Not scared are you?"

Paddy laughed. "Not bloody likely, so long as she don't hit out at me." He screwed up his eyes and looked down at Smallwood. "They say it's your blood she's after."

Smallwood thought of his immersion in the Cut. "So long as we get the bridge built first," he said shortly. "Come on now, business; and tell Polly to go to hell next time she calls."

He was leaning against the low wall at the back of the hut and was holding a heavy spanner picked up from the pile of blocks where it had been left by a careless workman. Suddenly a cutting rap across the knuckles made him drop it so that it fell into the water.

"Sod," he muttered, thrusting the hurt hand under an arm-pit.

The Irishman looked quizzical. "Polly?" he said.

"Sod Polly," said Smallwood withdrawing his hand; the blue of a painful bruise was beginning to show already.

"If I'm the villain I'd better keep out of the way," he said ruefully. "I'll telephone you each morning at nine and you can ring me at the office if anything crops up. You and Miller should be able to cope from now on." Miller was the contractor who left most of the work to his capable foreman while he sat on Boards, attended meetings and negotiated for further contracts.

Smallwood left and decided to locate Miss Christie.

"You'll have to make an appointment," said the clerk at the entrance counter in the small dingy house with 'Welfare and hours of opening' printed on a card in one of the windows. He thought she had an office in the palatial corridors of the new County Hall but was informed that she only 'borrowed' an office there for certain interviews.

"I'm the consultant surveyor. Tell her I've come about the North brothers," he said irritably and peremptorily.

The girl – she looked no more than seventeen thought Small-wood scathingly – stood firm.

"I'm sorry, she cannot be disturbed, her orders." (Not even 'sir' he noted – little upstart.)

"I'll come back in an hour. Please see that Miss Christie is informed. My card.'' He wrote on the back and left it on the counter.

He didn't return. He had intended to, but there were messages on his office desk, two of which required decisions and answers, and, when he consulted his watch, an hour and a half had passed. ''Blast – I'll telephone.''

''Miss Christie has had to go out on business. She said that she'd telephone on return.'' No apologies; he was honest enough to appreciate her application to work.

''What about the North brothers; did she leave a message about them?''

''Sorry, no. She said she would telephone.''

There was nothing to be done. He looked at his bruised hand and speculated. He left the office at 5.30 p.m., there had been no call from Miss Christie; he idly wondered whether she had a first name.

At 9 a.m. the following day he rang Paddy. ''All in order?'' he asked.

There wasn't an immediate reply, then, ''Th'ould woman's hard at it. When are the old men being shifted?''

''What's wrong?'' Smallwood's tone was sharp; he wanted to hear about the piling not about Polly's activities.

''The men aren't best pleased,'' shouted Paddy. Smallwood held the phone away from his ear. ''That young woman come down yesterday, that bitch of a dog jumped her and took a piece out of her leg, real nasty. They heard the tapping all day; got some of them worried.''

''I'll come over,'' said Smallwood. ''Get the men busy on the piling.'' He pushed a heap of paperwork into the 'in' tray, made for the door, paused, then decided to ring Miss Christie's number. The same cool voice, ''Sorry, Miss Christie is not in. Can I take a message?''

''Smallwood here. Any message for me?''

''Miss Christie had an accident. She hasn't been in. Sorry.''

''I know about the accident. Where is she?''

''She's still in the County Hospital. I think she'll be home today.''

Home, so she had a home. Smallwood was suddenly curious to know where 'home' was; but no time now to find out.

''Thanks,'' he said after a pause. He put down the receiver and shrugged on his duffel coat – still a cold wind even in June.

The piling was started. The noise of the pile driver would soon obliterate any tappings, real or imaginary. Paddy was on the towpath directing operations.

"Bad bit of bank here," he said as Smallwood approached. "It's going to take a few ton of concrete to firm that up. Mud, then clay. Trouble, too, back at the yard; lorry drivers reckon they'll strike."

"That's all we need," but Smallwood was resourceful. "Get the stuff on site as soon as possible. Randal the farmer will let us use his field." Randal was the farmer who had insisted upon his rights of access although he seldom, if ever, used the by-road.

"Bit swampy there with the river," Paddy observed. "I'll do me best." He looked gloomy but the work was progressing and there seemed no need to stay.

"I'll be up the road for an hour if you need me."

Charles was hardly more amiable than Paddy.

"You'll leave a good channel for the boats when the old house comes down?" he asked.

"I told you, yes. No problem. One-way traffic for a time, that's all. Same as the road traffic."

"Bad for business," said Charles. "Lots of new hire firms starting up too. Bad timing."

Smallwood was irritable. "You've known about the bridge for the last six months – no complaints before." He bit on his lower lip; no need to be shirty with Charles. "Come and have a pint," he added. "I could do with one."

A party of motorists, three men and a well-dressed woman filled the bar with smoke and loud brittle laughter. In a corner with a pint before him sat Bert North.

"Such a character," said the woman for all to hear, including old Bert. Smallwood regretted coming but there was no escape. The landlord hailed Charles.

"How's business?" he asked. "Not much traffic on the Cut this week. All going north I guess."

"A couple of boats not out but booked for the weekend. Not bad, could be worse." He ordered while Smallwood stood squarely with his back to Bert. What could you say to the old guy?

"Hullo there, Bert. I see you're well supplied." Charles breezed over to Bert's corner with a couple of pints and Smallwood was forced to follow.

Bert eyed him over the froth of the beer as he took a long silent pull at the drink.

"Hello, Mr North. How's your brother?" he asked.

"The dog got her yesterday," said Bert setting down the glass. "Never touched anyone before. Sorry it was her; she's all right."

"She's in hospital," said Smallwood coldly. The malevolent stare soured his drink. "Have to go back to the site," he said, standing.

"Finish your drink first then," said Charles. "Don't let old Bert here put you off."

Bert said nothing and Smallwood drank off his beer still standing.

"How's the new bridge going?" asked the barman through the smoke. The motorists were making a noisy exit.

"Fine," said Smallwood briefly.

"Our Will's coming tomorrow," said Bert.

"Your nephew, the solicitor from London?" asked Charles, not looking at Smallwood, who deferred his intended exit. Bert nodded and fixed his eyes upon Smallwood.

"He's coming to sort out t'bridge. Poll won't have us put out," he added.

The barman, Charles and Bert were all looking at Smallwood – waiting. "For what?" he thought. They were all against him, hostile. He was the interloper, the cause of their unease, uncertainty, the focus of their credulous belief that dead blind Polly would defeat him, would protect the cottage and her brothers, would check and foil his project to build the new bridge. They belonged here, he was a stranger. Even Charles looked faintly aggressive, had aligned himself with the brothers. "Sod them all," he thought.

"Be seeing you," he said as he turned away from them towards the door.

Charles caught up with him. "Not to worry," he said. "The nephew's a sensible young man; interested in the money under the mattress I guess. As for blind Poll . . . well, a few raps can't hurt you." Smallwood thought of his bruised hand; he didn't show it to Charles who might take it too seriously. He had been careful to keep on an old cotton glove whilst in the pub.

"I suppose there *is* no other way is there, Ken?" The older man knew that Smallwood had sensed his hostility back in the bar, and he wanted to restore the easy camaraderie he had previously established with this competent and energetic young man. He set great store on his ability to get on well with all those he met through his business, whatever their background. A 'Mr Everyman' he called himself, to himself. His teacher wife had found the pseudonym ridiculous and irritating; he'd taken care not to repeat it except to himself.

"Every possibility was checked and re-checked before the final decision was made. You know that." Smallwood was annoyed by the patronage. "Piling has started. I'll be seeing you," and he strode off down the road leaving Charles at the entrance to the marina.

"Right little Hitler – the way he walks, too."

Smallwood leaned over the bridge. The work was progressing, Paddy's red hair gleamed in the sunlight. A lorry with a concrete mixer brushed by and pulled in at the entrance to the field adjacent to the canal. All was well.

"Good for Paddy," he thought, "capable bloke."

He returned to the office. "Anything for me?" he asked the secretary in the adjoining cupboard of an office." Nothing from the Welfare Department? Get Miss Christie on the phone," as she shook her head and leafed through a pile of papers on her desk. She looked tired, middle-aged and colourless, a machine for operating a typewriter. Smallwood hardly knew her name, called her 'Miss' and wasn't even aware when occasionally she changed her hairstyle or her colour scheme. She was efficient, that was all he required.

"Nothing here, Mr Smallwood, and no phone message."

"Damn them," he thought. When was the eviction date? Why couldn't he be informed? No communication; self-important little empires.

"Get Miss Christie's office on the phone," he repeated. Time he was put in the picture about the old boys.

"Miss Christie is still in hospital," said the cool voice at the other end.

"Put me on to someone who is arranging for the transfer of the North brothers. The matter is urgent." He spoke brusquely.

"Mr Peterson has the matter in hand," said the voice.

"Then why the hell hasn't he contacted me?"

"I think there has been a hitch in the proceedings. I'll put you through to Mr Peterson. Hold on a minute please."

Smallwood had meant to ask after Miss Christie but the receiver was down at the other end before he could do so.

"Just the man," breezed in a new voice. "Mr Smallwood, isn't it? Could you possibly spare a few minutes? Someone here you'd like to meet. Office third on the right down the corridor in New Block – through the subway. Ask at the desk. Peterson, Chris Peterson. See you then." And the line went dead before Smallwood could even reply. "Impertinent bastard," he thought, but could hardly ignore the summons; for that's what it had been; not a request, an invitation, an enquiry, but a summons. Bloody Welfare.

"Miss, get me a coffee." He'd keep Mr bloody Peterson waiting. He looked out of the window over the rooftops to the new shopping precinct; the secretary came in with the coffee.

"I thought Welfare was housed in that old building down Temple Street," he said to the bringer of coffee.

"Yes, that's right. Miss Christie works from there most of the time."

"Then what's this office in New Block. A Mr Peterson?" he enquired turning to the coffee. She was on her way through the door to the adjacent nest-box.

"Mr Peterson, he's the new man. 'Miss Christie's number one' he calls himself."

"Why doesn't he work in Temple Street?"

"I don't really know, sir." The voice was sharp behind the lips moist with lipsalve. "Not enough room for him in Temple Street I expect. I think the whole of Welfare is due to move into New Block when it is finished." She left him to warm his hands round the generous mug of coffee; the coldest June for decades.

He took his time, wrote a couple of letters and then made his way over to New Block.

"Mr Peterson? Oh yes, sir," said the uniformed attendant at the enquiry desk. "Second floor, turn right, third door down on the right. Have you an appointment?"

"Wrong way round," thought Smallwood wryly. "Should have asked me that first."

"Yes, he's expecting me," and made for the stairs, no point in waiting for a lift. He'd forgotten he was on basement level and the climb to the second floor was an unnecessary exertion which added to his irritation.

"Come," said the breezy voice as Smallwood knocked and opened the door at the same time.

"Ah, Smallwood, just in time." There was a bland, youthful looking face smiling at him; the eyes over the rimless glasses did not smile however, noted Smallwood.

"Good of you to spare the time. We haven't met, have we?" Peterson stood and extended a hand across the desk and waved Smallwood to the chair opposite. "Ah yes, I saw you at the Rotarians last month; no time to be introduced but Jerry Gresham pointed you out." Jerry Gresham, the Chairman of the Board, so that was how it was. No wonder Miss Christie was so coldly competent. He shrugged at his impressions as Peterson signed a couple of papers. She'd not win anyway; hadn't a hope against the 'old boy' business; plucky to keep her end up though.

"Miss Christie," he asked, "how is she?"

"Poor girl," said Peterson; Smallwood's eyes narrowed at the condescension. "Shouldn't have gone there. Finds it hard to delegate; but now of course she has no choice. You can't run a busy office from a hospital bed."

"How is she?" repeated Smallwood.

"Out and about in a few days I shouldn't wonder. Nasty gash though. Mr North, can you come through now," he called to an open doorway which led to an inner office.

Smallwood did not register surprise; he knew that Peterson's eyes were upon him. As he had drunk his coffee slowly back in his office he had speculated upon the possible reasons for the summons to Peterson's office. It could only be something to do with the North brothers. "A hitch," the secretary had said. It had to be the solicitor nephew from London; Charles and Bert had warned him; there could be no other reason. The half-open door to the inner room, Peterson making him wait while he flourished a couple of signatures; his tactics were pretty obvious.

"Hopes to score off me." Smallwood's dislike turned to contempt. "Careful though," he thought. "He's the sort to get on; could be dangerous." He remained seated as Peterson rose again to introduce the dark, sharp-eyed man in the doorway. There was no mistaking who he was; Bert North all over again.

"Mr Will North – Mr Smallwood," said Peterson, beaming large teeth at each in turn.

"The solicitor from London," said Smallwood noting the same sharp ferrety eyes, a neat moustache on the sallow skin, well-cut dark suit, confident, wary.

"There's a small matter to discuss about the future of Mr North's uncles in the Bridge Cottage," said Peterson seating himself and spreading large hands so that the heavy gold ring on his little finger clanked audibly on the desk top. Presiding at a meeting? He had the mannerisms already. North sat in an upholstered chair also facing Smallwood and opened a briefcase.

"A hitch in proceedings, I understand," said Smallwood abruptly; he'd take the offensive if Peterson had decided to play games. He addressed himself entirely to North who looked as if he were prepared to be business-like and direct.

"I'm concerned about my uncles." North put his selected papers on a corner of the desk, ready. "When Mr Peterson kindly informed me of the proposed eviction I thought it necessary to check on the legalities. No doubt full enquiries were made from your office also."

"The property belongs to British Waterways Board and permission to demolish the cottage was obtained; the usual negotiations about compensation." Smallwood knew that there were no problems on that score; the deeds had been checked, final permission documented and completed.

"The cottage was built in 1910," continued Will North. "Original 'deeds' of the cottage – a copy of the page from one of the Grand Junction Canal's ledgers." He pushed over an insignificant sheet of faded foolscap paper, lined and with a brief entry in barely visible ink; signed, dated, with a rough seel, the outline of GJC just discernible. Smallwood waited. Will's ferrety eyes looked up shrewdly under the heavy eyebrows. "It reads, Mr Smallwood, 'Permission to build lengthman's cottage on the Heyford stretch southwards of the Globe Inn'. The rest isn't important – details of size and number of rooms."

He extracted another sheet from those on the table: "Copy of a record of completion and registration also from the Grand Junction's records handed over to the present British Waterways Board in 1948 when the canals became nationalized. You will have checked all this I'm sure," he commented.

Peterson leaned back in cheerful anticipation of the punch line; he thrived on the discomfiture of others, but was ignored by the two protagonists. Smallwood was wary. What loop-hole could he have left unchecked? His mind raced over the details; lease? ground rent? He could think of nothing but obviously the 'hitch' was there somewhere. He waited.

"Unfortunately, for you at least," continued North selecting a further sheet of lined ledger paper, "there is an earlier entry in a previous ledger still held by BWB and corroborated by a writ of possession still held at Lyalls in town."

Smallwood knew of Lyall and Lyall, an old established firm of solicitors in town, but he was still mystified. There had been no doubt about the ownership of the cottage.

"It's the coal wharf."

Peterson scrutinized the nails of his right hand. "The coal wharf," he repeated.

"You mean the length of coping overgrown with bushes?" asked Smallwood. "What about it?"

"It doesn't belong to the Waterways Board. It belongs to my uncles. If you pull down the cottage you still cannot trespass" – and he slightly emphasized the word – "upon the coal wharf without their permission."

A cackle of laughter seemed to invade the silence which followed. Smallwood had no doubt that Polly was enjoying the joke.

Will North's dry laugh was almost friendly. "Sorry, Mr Smallwood, but if you evict my uncles and demolish the cottage you will appreciate the implications."

"What proof have you?" It was an empty question but Smallwood was taking no chances.

"My old grandmother was a shrewd one," explained North. "She ran the coal business for years. She bought half an acre of land from the local farmer, the present Randal's great-great-uncle, with a small sum left to her when her mother died. She couldn't afford to build a house and for eight years lived in a boat moored alongside. My two uncles were born in that boat although only my uncle Jack remembers it. *My* father was a good deal younger," he explained. "That was back in 1902 when she was only twenty-three – old in those days of course. Her husband was employed by the Grand Junction. Then, in 1910, she sold part of the site to the company on which to build a cottage for a lengthman. With the money she bought a pair of boats. Grandfather came off the boats to take the job of lengthman and grandmother's boats, *Amy* and *Rose*, were run by Job and Ben, two of grandmother's brothers. They built up a good coal business between them and grandmother did all the business side, very capably, although I understand that she could neither read nor write."

"I thought that your uncles, Bert and Jack North, had lived in Bridge Cottage only for the past ten years," Smallwood remarked. "They were moved into it from the cottage up by the bridge on the A5."

"That's true," replied Will North, continuing the family history. "When my uncles left school they went to work on the boats."

"Your grandmother's boats?"

"No, grandmother was a tough old character; she thought they'd work better for a comparative stranger, and bring in some money as well. When her husband died my Uncle Jack applied for the job of lengthman so that they could continue to live in the tied cottage. He wanted to get married soon afterwards and to install his intended wife in part of the house. I don't know what happened but there was a dreadful row. Uncle Jack didn't get married; he and Bert and their sister Polly went to live in Globe Cottage. For some reason grandmother was allowed to continue living in Bridge Cottage until she died in 1951. My father lived there with her but was sent to a good school with money she had made from the coal business. Aunt Polly kept house for her brothers but they had nothing to do with grandmother and father; both sides completely ignored each other for years. When grandmother died, for all her business acumen, she left no will so that Jack, as the eldest, inherited the yard and the business. But they continued to live in Globe Cottage until it was pulled down, as you know, and to use the yard for the coal round, the coal all coming by road instead of in boats for many years now."

"And your father?" asked Smallwood.

"Went to university – took a degree in history – then went into road haulage. Died soon after grandmother. His wife, my mother, left him while I was still quite young. I went to boarding school but spent holidays with grandmother in the cottage.

There, now you have it, the family history; to indicate to you the claim my uncles know they have upon the yard – the house too, I guess, historically if not legally."

Smallwood knew that he was up against a century of local history; but, legally too, he knew he was beaten. It would be impossible to build the bridge or even to demolish the cottage without trespassing on the coal wharf. He knew he'd never get the required permission.

"Seems as if Polly wins," he said half to himself.

"Polly is grandmother's daughter," said Will with almost a smile. "She keeps me in order, too. Sorry, Mr Smallwood, I hope you find a solution."

"The bridge has a bad crack," replied Smallwood. "Something will have to be done."

"A solution to every problem," said Peterson, thankful that it wasn't his particular problem. His problem – Miss Christie was now out of the picture – had been neatly solved by this sharp-eyed little solicitor. Fancy having those two old characters for uncles; lucky he came down to sort it all out. Imagine them in the Senior Citizens' Precinct; what an escape. Jerry would be pleased; he'd tell him over a pre-lunch whisky at the Golden Feather tomorrow; informally of course.

His geniality filled the room. He almost went to the wall-cupboard for the glasses and good sherry he kept for certain people; but the case was settled. He'd not meet with Will North again and Smallwood wasn't likely to have any real influence where it mattered; cool sort of customer anyway – not his sort.

"Thanks for your time, Smallwood," he said in a tone of dismissal.

"I'll see Miss Christie when she returns," said Smallwood curtly. "Good morning, Mr North . . . Peterson," as he reached the door. He walked back to the office; another report to write, factual: "The ownership of the coal wharf by the brothers Jack and Bert North . . . etc." He'd leave the embroidery to Peterson. A message on his desk informed him that Paddy wanted him to phone, urgently.

"Bloody strike – no lorries – no deliveries – man's leg ripped by iron spike in water – men working slowly – bad feeling about the cottage."

When Paddy drew breath Smallwood replied, "Operations

suspended. Keep the piling going, necessary in any case for the bank. I'll be down directly. A legal hitch," he added to the explosives at the other end.

He rang Miller, wrote his brief report to the Chairman of the Board, with copies for the Social Services Department (Miss Christie) and the Waterways Board. He felt curiously relieved that it was over. He might well lose his job but thought it unlikely; the Waterways Board official was responsible for the error. He'd have to reassess the situation, there would have to be another solution. Rebuild the old bridge? Site a new one on the further side of the cottage? At least the brothers would be left in peace with the rats and their overgrown coal yard. Polly would be appeased. The solicitor would return to London. Miss Christie could direct her time and energy to other urgent cases.

He drove down to the site; Miller and Paddy awaited him in the site office, friendly and relaxed to his surprise.

"Can't be helped. One of those things. What next?" asked Miller. He'd done well in the building boom of the last few years, wanted to keep in with the Council and could afford to be flexible. "Lorry drivers on strike. We can afford to let them stay out for a few weeks; an ill wind . . . Come on, let's have a pint to celebrate." He was very sure of a new contract, thought Smallwood. Well, why not?

The men were sitting in the hedge, out of the wind; the sun was warm; newspapers, thermos, sandwiches. Two had already gone up the road to the Globe; Smallwood, Paddy and Miller followed. Charles was there as well. The news had spread and Smallwood was suddenly the popular centre of their friendly sympathy.

"Sorry old chap – an ill wind – Polly'll be pleased, never get the better of her – plenty of other ways," and the pints flowed freely and the suggestions for the bridge grew more numerous and improbable. Smallwood thought briefly of his last visit; hostility, suspicion, evasion. Now they were all with him.

"Not that I made the decision," he thought cynically, "I'd have gone ahead."

The door opened for Bert North and his nephew. "Thought we might find you all here," said the younger man. "Drinks on us this time and Uncle Bert pays."

The old man cackled. "You'll have to lend us a fiver, young Will, just until I get me pension."

The new bridge finally had to be built and the only place possible was just below the old one which had to be pulled down; subsidence made any hope of repair impossible. The job was long and tedious; unforeseen problems were constant; but Smallwood almost enjoyed the challenges, coped with the technicalities and the men. The unofficial strike was settled in days. Paddy's allegiance was reflected in the formula, "Mr Smallwood says", which he used as the final arbitrage in any difference of opinion with the men or even with his boss.

The actual reason for the change of plan was known only to a few; mostly it was thought that Smallwood had softened, had relented about evicting the brothers and that with great difficulty had succeeded in persuading the Councillors to rebuild the bridge on the more difficult site. Neither Smallwood nor old Bert proffered any other explanation. Charles went along with popular opinion until this was the story he accepted and retold many times; he had in fact known about young Will and the coal wharf. He liked to think well of everyone and was relieved that Smallwood was now accepted favourably in the locality. "He'd never have put the old boys out," he rationalized, "he's not so tough as he thinks he is."

Once or twice Smallwood reminded him. "They own the coal wharf, remember? That's why they're still there." In the end he gave up, shrugged and accepted the easy geniality; people would always believe what they wanted to believe, and his insistence upon the truth would only seem perverse and would irritate and antagonize those who now wished him well with the building of the bridge.

The Council meeting went smoothly too. Smallwood had been prepared for criticism, for hard accusations, even for statements of no confidence in his work, his inattention to detail. He was prepared; reports, records, propositions, costings, the whole span of logistics. He had worked unremittingly during the intervening week between the submission of reports from himself and Will North and the reconvening of the Council members to decide upon further action. The almost friendly smiles and nods of several individuals as they entered the room surprised him; his own hard eyes barely softened in return. They were upon the empty seat opposite. In the press of work he had almost forgotten her, had neglected to call on her or even to phone about her welfare. She'd be pleased about the turn of events. She didn't arrive and the benign Peterson took her place. Hard eyes met hard eyes, a slight query in Smallwood's.

"Miss Christie suggested that I should represent her as I was already involved," said Peterson, leaning across to speak to Smallwood through the subdued hubbub of talk.

"How is she?"

"Back on the job; busy as ever with her cases."

"I bet she is," thought Smallwood, "while you sit in meetings and be 'seen' in the right places."

"A little lame, but she'll be all right."

There was no opposition to the proposed plan to site the new bridge on the further side of the old one, although the cost would be increased by another few thousand pounds. Farmer Randal agreed to the re-routing of his access road and to the continued use of his land for storing materials and machinery – with adequate compensation. The old Urban Councillors added their support. Just one raised the question; what about the bend on the canal?

"It will be more acute. The canal will need to be widened by twelve feet to allow full-length boats to negotiate. There will need to be warning signs. The area engineer has agreed in principle if we meet the costs."

Smallwood had expected this to be the stumbling block. Again to his surprise it was eased over and agreed upon. He shrugged to himself; Rotarian dinners no doubt, the area engineer, the Chairman, other influentials . . . Peterson? Well, it eased his path. He wondered as he listened again to the Chairman's summing up just what had influenced the Councillors so positively in his favour; sentiment for the old boys? Or relief that their new SCs' complex would not be invaded by the blemish the brothers would make upon the sterile conformity of the occupants? Bert shaking hands with the Mayor; he almost smirked at the thought.

The construction of the re-sited bridge took almost a year instead of the proposed three months of the original plan. There were further problems of subsidence, of flooding from the nearby river and leakage from the further side of the canal into a pig yard. The pile-up of boats at each end of the narrow channel left for passage-way occurred almost daily to the continued enjoyment and then harassment of the workers. The footings of the old

184

bridge began to slip and constantly had to be shored up. Traffic had to be re-routed; a hard winter made work impossible for days and sometimes a week or two at a time. Yet, despite the delays, difficulties, frustrations, the work went comparatively smoothly; no strikes and a good feeling of camaraderie amongst the team under the energetic Paddy. Smallwood was kept busy elsewhere for much of the time but was at the site as often as possible. Old Bert even looked up from his bit of garden when he passed.

"Hello there, Mr North, how's your brother?" was Smallwood's usual greeting whenever he saw the old boy.

"Fair enough. How's the bridge?" Bert would answer. They met occasionally in the Globe and Smallwood fell into the habit of buying Bert his pint. Charles grew rather anxious about the pile-ups and the narrowness of the passage but was soon appeased when his claims for compensation were favourably met by the Council.

"Haven't heard Polly around lately," he said one day as he brought over three pints, himself, Bert and Smallwood.

The crafty eyes looked over at Smallwood.

"Poll's dead," he said, "over ten years ago. She ain't around no more." And that was all Smallwood heard of the tappings. Often he thought he had imagined it all except that there remained a sensitive strip across the back of his right hand where the bruise had long since disappeared.

He rubbed the place lightly as he leaned over the wall where he had first felt the hard rap which had caused him to drop the spanner. The wall and the old bridge were ready for demolition and Smallwood felt a cursory pang of regret for the old stonework; the concrete of the new bridge was sterile and featureless – like all new buildings he thought. A black and white cat was crouched among the grasses at the water's edge, hunting no doubt. It looked up from the concentration of its intent, alerted by the sound which reached Smallwood's ears seconds later.

He stiffened as he heard the tap, tap of the stick; he thought to have heard the end of it; what the hell was the matter with Blind Polly now? The tapping came up the rise which was just out of sight round the bend of the bridge.

"Well, Mr Smallwood." He spun round. Miss Christie stood there leaning on a stout walking stick. He hadn't seen her for months and it was now spring again. "Sorry, did you think it might be Polly?"

Smallwood grinned; good teeth; made him look young. "Perhaps you were Polly all the time," he said.

"Bert's dog managed to make a tear in the muscles of my calf," she explained. "It took a long time to heal and I still find the stick necessary. I admit though that I did a 'Polly' coming up the road just now. I saw your car by the office and guessed you might be taking a look at the old bridge."

She wasn't wearing the spectacles.

"When I've been visiting the brothers I've almost felt like Blind Polly at times – almost," and she smiled back at him.

"Come and have some lunch," said Smallwood.

"Thanks Ken, I'd love to," she replied, "and my name is Noelle. Come and meet my mother, although I think you must know her by sight – she's on the Education Committee."

They moved off together over the bridge and the cat returned to its vigilance in the long grass.